SOMEONE ALWAYS KNOWS

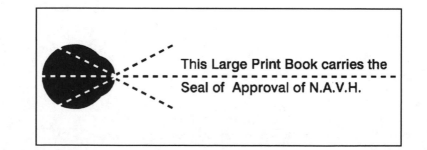

This Large Print Book carries the
Seal of Approval of N.A.V.H.

SOMEONE ALWAYS KNOWS

MARCIA MULLER

THORNDIKE PRESS

A part of Gale, Cengage Learning

Farmington Hills, Mich • San Francisco • New York • Waterville, Maine
Meriden, Conn • Mason, Ohio • Chicago

GALE
CENGAGE Learning®

LIBRARY OF CONGRESS CATALOGING-IN-PUBLICATION DATA

Names: Muller, Marcia, author.
Title: Someone always knows / by Marcia Muller.
Description: Large print edition. | Waterville, Maine : Thorndike Press, 2016. |
   Series: A Sharon Mccone mystery | Series: Thorndike Press large print mystery
Identifiers: LCCN 2016020173 | ISBN 9781410484093 (hardcover) | ISBN 1410484092
   (hardcover)
Subjects: LCSH: McCone, Sharon (Fictitious character)—Fiction. | Women
   detectives—California—Fiction. | Large type books. | GSAFD: Mystery fiction.
Classification: LCC PS3563.U397 S64 2016b | DDC 813/.54—dc23
LC record available at https://lccn.loc.gov/2016020173

Published in 2016 by arrangement with Grand Central Publishing, a division of Hachette Book Group, Inc.

Printed in the United States of America
1 2 3 4 5 6 7 20 19 18 17 16

For Bill, with love

■ ■ ■ ■

MONDAY,
OCTOBER 5

■ ■ ■ ■

11:12 a.m.

"It's awfully different from the artist's rendering," I whispered to my nephew Mick Savage.

He and I and several of my staff were standing at the spacious entrance to the recently remodeled McCone & Ripinsky building on New Montgomery Street in San Francisco's financial district. Workmen had just removed the tarps from a sculpture we'd commissioned — at great cost — from the world-renowned artist Flavio St. John.

"What do you suppose Flavio's intention was?" Julia Rafael had recently been dating a prominent Latino painter and was into all things artistic.

"He needed a cure for a hangover," Patrick Neilan offered, scratching at his thatch of red hair.

"Don't be facetious," I said. "What is it supposed to be?"

9

"Looks like clamshells." This from our office manager, Ted Smalley. "A cheap concrete clamshell fused to a larger fake gold one. Flavio must've been hungry for seafood the day he came up with the design."

The workmen with the tarps seemed anxious to pack up and go. A small crowd had gathered, blocking their trucks.

"Where *is* Flavio?" I asked.

"Rome," Patrick said. "He had urgent business there, so I drove him to the airport the other night."

"Urgent business? Without letting me know he was leaving? More likely he was escaping the scene of the crime — with our check in his wallet. I'm putting a stop on it."

"Ma'am," a gentleman in the growing crowd said, "can you explain why you people elected to put such an eyesore on your beautifully restored granite building?"

"Well," I began, "we thought . . . the concept is as —"

"As ugly as my aunt Stella Sue's butt."

That came from my husband, standing on the edge of the crowd: tall, lean in his tight jeans, with the brim of his cowboy hat pulled down over his roughly hewn face. People erupted into laughter at his remark.

Trying not to laugh myself, I said, "The

10

gentleman who just spoke is my partner and co-owner of the building, so I suppose he has a right to express his opinion." I shot Hy a dark look and added, "And you don't have an aunt Stella Sue."

He shrugged.

"You may as well come up here and say a few words."

He shouldered through the crowd.

"Actually, folks, I was just joking. The designer of this dramatic entrance, Flavio St. John, is one of the finest sculptors in the world. His talents in any form of sculpting surpass even those of the late Beniamino Bufano, who, except for that horror of a spire that looks like a totem pole at Timber Cove Inn up the coast, did all of us Californians proud."

I stepped on Hy's foot — hard.

He added, "Apparently our clamshells are Flavio's equivalent of Bufano's totem pole."

Then, mercifully, he shut up.

"Thanks for coming!" I called to the crowd, and turned to glare at Hy.

He backed up, holding his hands out defensively. "What could I say? It's a piece of shit."

"Of course it is." I took his arm and hustled him toward the door.

"We ought to sue that rat-faced little

11

bastard," he added.

"Keep your voice down."

"Crappy concrete and bogus gold that look like clamshells with chipped edges are *not* the way to inaugurate our new partnership."

"We'll do something about it."

"What? There's probably some goddamn clause in our contract with him that says we can't alter it without his permission."

"Then it'll just have to meet with an accident. A *terrible* accident."

"McCone, I love the way you think," he said as we entered the building.

Maybe I was just used to downscale, but many times when I came through the door of the high-security building — into the express line, where all the guards knew me — I felt as if I were sneaking in under false pretenses. The offices seemed to demand that I spiff up my public image: dress more stylishly, use more artfully applied makeup, and for Christ's sake get those nails done!

All this paranoid hoopla induced by a *building*! One owned by my husband's company and, since we'd merged our firms, by me too.

We entered the reception area on the second floor, and I spotted a freshly opened bottle of champagne and several glasses on the desk. I looked at my watch: it was after noon. Why not? I needed a drink.

In the area beyond the desk, staff members were milling around, their faces studies in shock and disbelief. Most were imbibing wine in quantity. In spite of my outrage over Flavio St. John's ridiculous sculpture, I couldn't help but take pleasure in seeing all the people — new hires, old-timers, and friends.

Since the merger, there had been quite a few changes: Hy and I consulted on all cases together. Mick had hired more tech people, many of whose activities I couldn't fathom; they populated the third floor below us. Ted had also hired a large support staff, some of whom I suspected were practically living in the building — at least I'd seen many sleeping bags, duffels, and clothing on hangers in the second-floor hallways. Sometimes in the dark hours of the morning I worried about the city finding us out and trying to levy a hotel tax or maybe penalize us for violating some ordinance. They'd been closing in on such home-sharing services as Airbnb and VRBO. But recently our rate of closed cases had climbed steadily, and our employees were compensated well enough that they could relocate if necessary. So who was I to complain about a few squatters?

I accepted a glass of champagne from Ted and tapped on the desk. Everyone quieted and turned to me. I toasted them. "Here's to Italian sculpture, twenty-first-century style."

Many laughed, but others — especially those who had been involved with the designer of the new façade — looked as if they'd rather be at their desks preparing their résumés.

"Come on," I said, "it's not the end of the world. We made some mistakes and were too trusting, that's all."

Ted moaned, "Why did we allow Flavio to keep his 'art' covered up until today? Why didn't we sneak looks at it instead of unveiling for everybody to see?"

"Because we were caught up in the mystique — which Flavio wove all too well — of 'great artists must be allowed to create in private.' "

"At least there weren't any press people there," Patrick said. "They'd be accusing us of destroying a perfectly beautiful building."

"Uh," Ted said, "there was one representative of the press —"

"Who?" I asked.

"Jill Starkey."

Oh, shit!

Starkey was a former *Chronicle* reporter

14

and owner/editor/sole employee of a dreadful right-wing rag called *The Other Shoe.* A terrible little troll — oh, I'd pay in my next life for thinking such things, assuming there was a next one, but right now I didn't care — Starkey had frizzy brown hair and a pinched lopsided smile, and hated most things (except for ice cream, and she wasn't too sure about that). One of the chief objects of her hatred was me.

I've never understood what I did to deserve such venom. When she was at the *Chron,* I'd been cordial to her, even though I hadn't really liked her. But since she'd been dismissed from the major paper for causing a libel suit that forced them to settle a large amount of money on the plaintiff, she'd found herself an investor and set up her own publication. Then the gloves had come off. Over and over she'd aimed journalistic jabs and punches at me that I'd learned to duck or roll with. It was either that or throw her off the Golden Gate Bridge.

Thank God *The Other Shoe* was a weekly; the next issue wouldn't come out till Friday.

Ted said, "You okay, Shar?"

"Yeah, just thinking about how much I dislike Jill Starkey."

"Me too. She's homophobic."

15

"I know. How does she find enough people in a city like this who will read her crap?"

"As your mother would say, there's a top for every box."

I smiled at the garbled expression. My mother has a new one almost every day. Sometimes I think she does it on purpose.

"Seriously, though, we've got to do something about that blight on the building's façade. This is one of the classics of its era."

Built in 1932, of carefully selected slabs of Vermont granite, the four-story office building has large float windows (as they called plate glass back then) that allow sun and moon and starshine to brighten its offices and corridors. The floors are made of beautifully tessellated hardwood, except on our fourth level, where a massive leak has necessitated carpeting. We lease the ground floor to stylish shops — leather goods, a high-end women's shoe store, the legendary Angie's Deli, and a sweetshop that I've been known to go around the block to avoid — and reserve two, three, four, and the roof garden for our growing operation. The real heart of McCone & Ripinsky is the fourth floor and the roof garden.

Fourth floor: picture a big, well-furnished waiting room with soft leather chairs and sofas, and rosewood tables covered with a wide variety of periodicals. Coffee, tea, you-name-it provided; drinks too if the client insists. I think we stocked yak's milk once for an extremely fussy client from the Middle East. And if any of them are hungry after long drives or international flights, Angie's Deli provides.

Sometimes I feel as if I'm running a catering service rather than an investigative agency. But then, I've been known to tack my food orders on to the clients'.

Back to the offices: as with the building, I have mixed feelings about them. They are elegant — very, very elegant. Oriental carpets over the hardwood on floors two and three; deeply piled pale-gray carpet on the fourth; something that lasts like Astroturf but seems more like real grass on the roof. Attractive and functional contemporary furnishings throughout; posters from special events at the city's museums brightening the pale-gray walls. My own space is a dream: it has an expansive view from the Golden Gate to the East Bay hills, a huge cherrywood desk and matching bookcases and file cabinets, and a full-length sofa so I don't have to lie on the floor during my infamous "quiet times" (which often are not quiet).

My ages-old armchair, years ago rescued

from my office in a closet under the stairs at All Souls Legal Cooperative, where I began my career, is now restored in leather; it and its newish matching hassock are positioned by the windows under a healthy potted schefflera plant named Mr. T., after Ted. The Grand Poobah, as he prefers to call himself, had decorated the suite single-handedly. Sometimes I regret giving him such a free hand and open checkbook with the remodeling, but he has impeccable taste, and the results attest to it.

Needless to say, I wasn't used to such luxurious working environs. For years my agency's offices were on the upper tier of Pier 24 1/2, which is now in the process of being demolished, and I'd loved it there, drafty and cold and echoing as it was.

Before that I'd first had the coat closet and then an upstairs room at All Souls Legal Cooperative's big Victorian in Bernal Heights, in the southeastern section of the city. The poverty law firm, headed by my best male friend, Hank Zahn, had subsisted in the big broken-down house, with some employees living in and others — mercifully, including me — living out. But most of the friendships forged there have carried on to this day, and when the co-op folded, I managed to bring Ted along to my new

18

agency. Hank and his wife and law partner, Anne-Marie Altman, have offices within two blocks of us. And the new people we've acquired so far seem to be good fits.

I didn't miss the old days, not really. But I wasn't used to such affluence. My family had been solvent, but just barely. I'd put myself through UC Berkeley on small scholarships and nighttime jobs as a security guard. The years after graduation were lean — who wanted a young woman with a BA in sociology? But then I'd gotten on with a private investigator, trained under my employer for my license, and landed the job with All Souls. After that things had slowly gotten better.

Finally I'd met Hy Ripinsky. Man with a shady past who possessed a great deal of money of an equally shady origin, or so I'd thought at the time. The secrets of that past and money we'd sorted out over time, and I'd finally come to trust him. A couple of times, literally, with my life. After we married, I'd realized I was a wealthy woman, in more ways than just financially.

I plunked my briefcase down on my desk, then studied it critically. It was getting shabby. I was having a bad hair day, and I realized that once again I'd forgotten to put on makeup.

Well, old habits die hard.

1:05 p.m.
Ted buzzed me. "You're not going to like this."

"What's the matter?"

"You and Hy have a visitor. Gage Renshaw."

My breath caught and my pulse elevated. ". . . Gage — that can't be! Hy and I assumed he died years ago."

"But you never received conclusive proof of it."

"No, but it's been years since he disappeared. Knowing Gage, he would've turned up to devil us long before this. Are you sure it's him?"

"Turn on your surveillance cam and take a look."

I touched the switch. The grainy picture on the monitor — not the best we should have bought — showed the reception desk; I moved the cursor to take in the rest of the room.

The figure slumped on the sofa was Gage Renshaw all right. Older, more rumpled than I remembered him, but still with that jet-black hair with a white shock hanging down over his Lincolnesque forehead.

"Son of a bitch," I said.

20

"What should I do with him?" Ted asked.

"Throw him off the roof garden."

"Come on, Shar, this is serious. He's smarmy and obnoxious as ever, and he's demanding to see both you and Hy."

I thought quickly. "Take him to the hospitality suite." A room off second-floor reception. "Offer him food, drink, whatever. Say Ripinsky and I are in conference, but we'll be with him shortly."

"Will do. You want surveillance cams activated there, right?"

"Yes." I cut the connection, and then buzzed Hy.

"I need you right away," I told him. "One of our worst nightmares has just come true."

Hy and Gage Renshaw went way back, to the days when they were both flying highly questionable passengers and cargo in Southeast Asia for an outfit called K-Air owned by a man named Dan Kessell.

As Hy had put it to me, he'd suspected but didn't want to know for sure what K-Air was involved in; the planes were delivered to the pilots fully loaded and they didn't even know their destinations until immediately before departure. There were a few times when he flew passengers concealed in the skin of the plane, meaning between the outer layer and the inside

21

cabin. A good place to freeze to death, as one of his human cargo did. He parachuted contraband into far-flung places. Fellow pilots disappeared into those places and were never seen again. It was a violent world, but he accepted it because he had very little to return to: his father, stepfather, and mother were dead; his stepfather had willed him a small sheep ranch in California's high desert country near Tufa Lake, the region where he'd been born but that was by no means home; he'd wandered for years, but never found a place that *was* home, and he assumed he never would.

The turning point came when his regular flight plan was changed by Dan Kessell, the owner of K-Air, from a city in Thailand called Chiang Mai to an abandoned village near the Laotian border. He was forced down into a clearing by one of his passengers — a drug lord — where he was forced to witness a horrible massacre. That was it — Hy decided to get out (get clean, he'd said) and return to the high desert country of California.

In the years that ensued, Hy became an environmentalist, married a fellow activist, and, when he lost his wife to multiple sclerosis, he sank into a manic-depressive state that alarmed even those friends who'd

22

always considered him a wild man. Then I had appeared and our life together, while sometimes tumultuous, usually had a settled quality that neither of us had experienced before.

Meanwhile, Renshaw and Kessell returned stateside and formed RKI, an international executive protection firm. Basically what such firms do in this era of terrorist threats is contract with US companies to provide security risk analysis, program design, and defensive training. They also have contingency services: crisis management, ransom negotiation and delivery, and hostage recovery. They lured back Hy into the firm as a hostage negotiator with promises of big bucks and short hours; the bucks flew in, but long hours persisted, because Hy is as driven as I am when he's on the trail of a solution to a crime.

Dan Kessell had been murdered a few years ago, his killer never apprehended. I had my suspicions about the murder, all of them involving Renshaw. Later, Renshaw had totally disappeared, probably because one of his nefarious ventures went sour, and after a suitable time Hy had petitioned the court and been granted sole ownership of what was first known as Ripinsky International and is now McCone & Ripinsky

International (an unfortunate appellation when it becomes MRI, conjuring up visions of X-ray rooms and white-coated technicians). But now it seemed Gage was back. And no doubt with plans intended to mess up the whole arrangement.

1:21 p.m.

I was on the phone with Hank Zahn, our primary attorney, when Hy burst into my office. I held up one finger and punched the speaker button. Hank's familiar voice filled the room.

"This is a situation I've never encountered before, Shar. When you and Hy transferred the ownership of RKI, did you have Renshaw declared legally dead?"

"I don't think so. That should be in your files."

"Well, it's not. Do you know who Mr. Renshaw's attorney is?"

"No. I doubt he has one. Gage and legality don't exactly mesh."

"I'm going to have to speak with some of my colleagues and do some research."

"How long will that take?"

"Depends. A few hours, anyway."

"And what the hell do I do with Renshaw while you're researching? He's already eating and drinking his way through our

24

hospitality suite." On the monitor I'd watched Gage order up two huge pastrami sandwiches, potato salad, a sixty-dollar bottle of Merlot, and a big chunk of chocolate cake from Angie's.

"Try to find out what he wants," Hank said. "If he won't tell you, make nice anyway. Check him into a good hotel — and later stick him with the bill."

Every now and then I really like lawyers.

1:37 p.m.

Hy was furious — white-lipped, eyes flashing, hands knotted into fists. When I showed him Renshaw on the video monitor, I was afraid he'd rip it off its mountings. I persuaded him to sit down and take several deep breaths before I said, "Okay, you heard Hank advise us to take a low-key approach to this."

"Why? I'd like to throttle the bastard. What d'you bet he wants in on the firm?"

"Then we pay him off. Everybody's got his price, and from the way he looks, I'd say Gage's is lower than most these days."

I watched Renshaw light a cigarette with a Bic, draw on it. After a moment he flicked ashes onto the table, missing the ashtray.

Slob.

Hy, considerably calmer, studied Renshaw

25

on the monitor. "You may be right. I spot a broken shoelace."

I buzzed Mick and asked him to show Renshaw in.

Up close he looked even seedier than he had on the monitor. When he shambled into my office I noted that his hair was unbarbered and the large white shock that hung over his forehead was greasy, and that he hadn't shaved today. His clothing, khakis and a blue shirt, were rumpled and worn. The raspy catch in his voice from smoking too much had worsened. His beat-up leather flight jacket I could understand: both Hy and I had ones like it; the more years you're a pilot, the more evidence of your prowess you want to exhibit, and — for whatever reason — a disreputable flight jacket is part of the mystique.

He spread his hands wide and said, "Here you see me in all my resurrected glory." Then he plunked himself down in one of the chairs that faced my desk and propped his feet on its edge. Yes, he did have a broken and badly knotted shoelace, and the heels and soles were worn down.

Hy took the other chair, and I retreated to mine.

"So, Gage," Hy said, "long time."

"You bet."

"What've you been doing with yourself?"

"This and that." With an annoyed gesture he pushed the shock of white hair off his forehead.

"How come you haven't been in touch?"

"No need to be." Then he looked around and added, "Nice operation you've got here."

"We like it," I said.

"Bringing in the big bucks. Nice house in the Marina, nice place on the Mendo coast. And Hy, I hear you've still got the ranch. Still got a plane too. And this firm has one of those CitationJets, if you need to get where you're going in a hurry."

"Where'd you get all this information?" Hy asked.

"You're a fine one to question me. We learned at the feet of the same father."

"What does that mean?" Hy asked.

"Father Mammon. He taught us the lure of the buck."

Hy's expression told me he had no patience for that kind of nonsense. He said, "What do you want, Gage?"

"What do I want?" He paused, rubbing his stubbled chin as if in thought. "What *does* Gage want? Well, at the moment he doesn't rightly know. Why don't you show me around this place?"

"It's off-limits to anybody but qualified personnel."

"You were always big on security, Ripinsky."

"It's paid off for me."

"For you, maybe." He stroked his chin again. "Not for me." Pause. "What *do* I want? Not an in with this agency, for sure. No action here. You've turned what was a great outfit into a bunch of wimpy yes-men. You still have the training camp down south? The safe houses?"

RI has always maintained various fully staffed dwellings throughout the country to provide for clients at risk. These range from pricey homes and condos to modest suburban tract houses to sleazy motels. I'd had the dubious privilege of hiding out in one of the worst in San Francisco, a former hot sheet motel near the Great Highway.

Hy said, "We have a number of safe houses, yes. We still own the camp, but we don't use it much any more."

The training camp is comprised of fifty-some acres, an airstrip, and a few classrooms and housing near El Centro in the Imperial Valley. It was originally used for teaching operatives and clients the tools of their trade: self-defense, evasionary driving tactics, firearms skills, hand-to-hand combat.

28

I'd been there only once, and encountered a horrible situation that had nearly cost Hy and me our lives. If I could help it, I'd never go back.

"Yeah," Renshaw said, "it looked kind of dead when I drove by there on my way up here. Where you sending the new ops now?"

"We outsource the training."

"Still, you oughta keep the place up. There're weeds growing through the asphalt on the runway. And the buildings look like shit."

I asked, "Where were you driving up from, Gage?"

"South."

"That's no answer."

"It's all you're getting."

I noted the word *up* on a legal pad. Renshaw glanced curiously at me, but didn't ask what I'd written.

"You want to buy the camp? We're putting it up for sale soon," Hy said. "You could start your own driver-training and stunt school."

"Ha. No way."

"Why not? You above all that now?"

They were likely to get off on an unnecessary and unproductive tangent, so I said, "Since you're so disparaging of the firm, Gage, and not legally entitled to any sort of

29

compensation" — God, that was what I hoped to hear from Hank later! — "just why did you come here?"

He shook his head slowly. "I can't articulate it."

"Try; I've never known you to be at a loss for words."

"But I am." He spread his upturned hands wide.

"Then why show up at all, unannounced, after so many years?"

"Maybe I'm sentimental, just wanted to catch up on old times."

"Well, it's been great, but . . ." I stood up.

Renshaw stood too. "Now that you've mentioned it, though, there just might be something I want from you old pals." He chuckled and then started for the door. "You folks'll be hearing from me soon, you betcha."

As soon as he was gone, I got on the intercom to Ted, asking him to put an immediate tail on Renshaw.

Then Hy and I conferred, deciding to set Mick and his department to work on a deep search into Renshaw's background. I knew surface details, but they were skimpy. Even Hy, who'd been acquainted with him for years, had little insight into Renshaw's past, and neither of us had so much as a glimmer into what he might have been doing since his disappearance.

The day had turned warm and cloudless, as so many do in October. Hy and I decided to continue our conversation on the roof garden. It was a lovely space: yew trees planted in big containers; flowers in smaller ones; plenty of comfy, cushioned redwood furniture to curl up on, plus a couple of round tables with umbrellas. Most important, it was protected from the wind and fog by huge Plexiglas panels.

While we awaited news about Renshaw, we went over and over what we knew of him.

Hy: I don't even know where he was born or anything about his family.

Me: I don't think that matters any more. He's not the type who would have kept in touch with anybody from his warm and fuzzy past.

Hy: Nothing new on him on Google. Just old stuff from RKI days.

Me: Mick may turn up something. He has his ways with the behemoth Internet.

Hy: Well, we know Renshaw was with the DEA, on that super-secret detail known as CENTAC. Even the higher-ups in the government didn't know about it.

Me: Well, that doesn't surprise me. Look at what the CIA concealed from the Obama administration.

Hy: After CENTAC was outed and then disbanded, Renshaw flew for a while in Thailand.

Me: And after he teamed up with Dan Kessell and formed RKI, he fell for my ruse about wanting to kill you.

I'd successfully bluffed Renshaw years ago, telling him I wanted to locate Hy so I could kill him. When I'd saved Hy, Renshaw had never forgiven me.

Ted came up the stairs and stuck his head out the door: Thelia Chen, he said, the operative who'd been tailing Renshaw, had lost him near Goat Alley. The block — colorfully named after the herds of goats that had once grazed peacefully in a pastoral pre–gold rush city — was in actuality a grimy, unpaved passageway ending at a brick wall off Natoma Street South of Market. I knew the territory, since I'd once conducted a long surveillance on an escaped prisoner who had sheltered there. No doors opened on the alley, and the narrow single exit — which Renshaw had apparently taken — came out at Mission, a busy thoroughfare with heavy foot traffic where a man could easily be lost in the crowds. I wished I'd conducted the tail job myself or asked Mick to assign it to someone more experienced than Chen, a former financial analyst with Wells Fargo who hadn't done much field-work.

"Seems as if Renshaw's as crafty as ever," I said to Hy. "He must've known we'd have him followed."

"He may be crafty, but he's not putting his skills to good use. Did you notice his clothes?"

"You know, their shabbiness might've been a way of disguising his real status. Why hint at anything that he doesn't want us to know?"

"Could be." Hy looked at his watch. "I'm out of here, have a meeting with a prospective client. Want to come along?"

"No, I've got plenty of work to catch up on here. See you at home for tacos later?"

"You got it."

3:33 p.m.
Hank called me back in the middle of the afternoon. "I've talked with several other attorneys about your problem with Renshaw, and they all agree that there's a legal precedent in your favor. His abandonment,

33

lack of communication . . . did you try to locate him?"

"Not very hard," I admitted.

"But you did try?"

"Sure. We're investigators, that's what we do." My voice had an edge to it.

"Don't get testy with me."

"Sorry, I didn't mean to. This has been an awful day."

"Well, hang in there. And send me any info on your or Hy's attempts to locate this pest."

I went back to my files. In the months since the agency merged with RI and expanded, it seemed paperwork — on real paper or the computer — had come to dominate my life. Whether here in the office or at home, my computers and iPhone fired off messages, reports, and complaints at me with incredible speed. I couldn't ignore the infernal devices; they rang and beeped at me with a persistence I'd never imagined any electronic device could exhibit. Sometimes I longed for the old days —

Well, maybe not. Computers, which I'd previously hated and vowed never to use, now provide all sorts of data with speed and accuracy. For a poor typist like me, the Delete key is of prime importance. Fax machines, cell phones, and high-quality printers allow me to cut through red tape and save time. And the Internet is a great research tool — if I don't take as gospel every word that appears on the screen. I still fact-check in person and with written sources, particularly the older ones, which tend to be more accurate. But the old days? Carbon copies, Wite-Out, endless erasing and retyping . . . uh-uh, not for me.

When I looked up from a particularly boring case report, I found it was full dark; the lights of the city shimmered before me in a way that I knew predicted cold temperatures for the days ahead. The thought of tacos nudged at me. Time to go home.

■ ■ ■ ■

TUESDAY,
OCTOBER 6

■ ■ ■ ■

8:57 a.m.

Mick looked through my office door and said, "I've compiled a list of people you may want to talk to about Renshaw." He handed me two printed sheets. "It's pretty extensive, many of them out of state or outside the country."

"Let me get Ripinsky in here."

As we waited for Hy, I studied my nephew. He looked good, fit and rested. If any traces of the problems he and his partner Alison had gone through earlier in the year remained, they weren't major ones. I was about to ask him how the painting on their new house on Potrero Hill was going when Hy came in. The three of us went over the list together.

I said, "In order to contact all these people, we're going to have to co-opt other agencies in the more far-flung locations."

"I don't think so," Hy told me. "RI's

39

people — I mean, our people can handle it. And since Renshaw has surfaced here, I'd hazard that he has a connection in the Bay Area." He looked a shade embarrassed: since we'd joined our firms, he sometimes slipped, speaking as if he were the sole owner of the organization.

I ignored the error — it didn't matter. "Right. But what's he been doing all these years?"

"Scamming," Mick said. "You'll notice the names on that list live all over the globe, but he primarily focused on South America, maybe because he's fluent in Spanish and Portuguese."

I looked at the list: Chile, Venezuela, Argentina, Brazil.

"What kinds of scams?" I asked.

"The usual — extortion, blackmail, you name it. In Venezuela he and the sixteen-year-old daughter of a high government official ran off together, taking a good bit of money she'd stolen from her father's safe; when officials found her and returned her to her parents, the money and Renshaw were gone. The brat had the nerve to proclaim to her family that he was 'the greatest fuck' she'd ever had."

I paused, thinking about that. In my opinion the young woman must've not had

40

many good fucks. Self-absorbed people like Renshaw are never very good in bed.

"Why didn't the girl's family prosecute?"

"She refused to testify. So they shipped her off to a convent instead. Renshaw speedily exited the country."

"When was that?" I asked.

"Two years ago. And that's the last trace of him before he came to this office yesterday."

That was interesting. Mick and his staff were the brightest and best in their area of expertise. If they couldn't find out what Renshaw had been up to recently, who could?

Again I studied the list. "Let's start by divvying up the locals among us."

We spent a long time breaking up the list, sorting the names by their locations to save driving time and legwork. Mick said he would assign Derek and Patrick to the city and Marin, and I opted for the Peninsula. Hy, who was currently juggling two cases, would assign other operatives if they became necessary and oversee the operation from the office.

My first choice of interviewees, Gil Stratton, president of Quick Stops, an air charter firm that Renshaw had once worked for, wasn't available till four fifteen that afternoon, but a late appointment was okay with me. Stratton was located at Mineta San José International, a good hour's drive down the Peninsula, and I really needed the time to plow through more paperwork.

11:43 a.m.
Before I could really get into it, however, Ted buzzed me. "A new client to see you."

I clicked my tongue in exasperation. "Who?"

"Name's Chad Kenyon."

At first the name didn't register. When it did, I said, "Mr. Kenyon's had dealings with Julia. Can't you pass him on to her?"

"He says he'll speak only with you."

Lucky me. The Kenyon brothers, fat Chad and skinny Dick, are a powerful, albeit not always a welcome, force in the city — indeed in most of the Western states. Their reputation is based on their penchant for buying and selling things with precision and speed. They snap up any object that appeals to them, not for its intrinsic value but because turning it quickly at a profit will illustrate their uncanny expertise.

A diamond brooch or a ruby necklace? Got plenty in inventory. Cameos? Harder to find, but we got this great pair of earrings and matching bracelet. Net . . . *what*? Oh,

42

netsuke. Those little Japanese carvings. You want a fish? Turtle? Butterfly? We can get it for you within the hour. Murano glass? Do we ever have a vase for you!

Canoes. Are you into them? We got an antique longboat, brought the ancient Hawaiians over from wherever the hell they started. No boats? Okay. How about financial instruments? We picked up these stocks at a fire sale price; they're kinda dogs, but a smart operator maybe could build on their history. Say, you know that big tract of land up north near Sawyer's Bar? The state and federal Bureau of Land Management had a falling out over how to use it, so we stepped in quick and now it's ours. Name the number of parcels you want.

None of the items they brokered were particularly important to the Kenyons; what mattered was the chases and negotiations. Not even the profits they gleaned seemed to interest them, although they'd made many millions and lived lavishly.

You would have thought you'd find the Kenyons seated at the top of San Francisco's social pyramid. After all, this is a town built upon often ill-gotten gold rush gains. Also, we're tolerant — some say too much so — of our eccentrics, scoundrels, and downright fools. However, we do, in the main, know how to carry on polite conversation and which utensils to use at the dinner table.

The Kenyons knew nothing of the niceties of life. They dressed loudly, ate hoggishly, and on one infamous evening had been caught by a wire services photographer throwing bouillabaisse at each other in a high-toned Roman bistro. Now, apparently, they were back.

I'd never met either brother, but Julia had, while we were investigating a cult-like group called the Night Searchers who carried out their rituals in a vacant lot belonging to the Kenyons. Her description of Chad as a man who could "gobble a whole steer and then ask for an ox," and the tape recording she'd made to prove it, made the prospect of a meeting with him less than appealing.

"Are you sure you can't send Mr. Kenyon along to Julia?" I asked.

"Nope. She's out working the Renshaw angle, and besides, Kenyon seems pretty insistent."

"All right, give me five and send him in," I said. And then, thinking of the famed Kenyon appetite, added, "And for God's sake, follow up with a tray of noshes."

Chad Kenyon's big body shook when he walked. His facial skin drooped in great

44

jowls. But to give him credit, kindness showed in his soft brown eyes, and the lines around them testified to much laughter. He was short — a little less than my own five foot six — but in spite of his excess padding, he carried himself well in his expensively tailored blue silk suit. Mercifully his handshake was firm — unlike the gorilla grips I'd recently noticed a lot of men employing.

I seated him in my conversation area and made small talk while Kendra Williams, Ted's assistant — whom he had dubbed the Paragon of the Paper Clips — served coffee and noshes. Kenyon looked the serving plate over with interest, then helped himself to an assortment of mini pizzas.

To be polite, I took a couple myself, then asked, "What can we do for you, Mr. Kenyon?"

"Please, call me Chad."

"And I'm Sharon."

He fiddled around with a leather card case, produced one, and laid it on my desk. "I asked to talk with you personally because Little Sweetheart says you're the best in the business."

"Who's Little Sweetheart?"

"Ms. Julia Rafael."

"Nice of her to say so. I assume you have

45

a problem."

"A big one." He grimaced. "I'm afraid things are going to get out of control if something's not done soon."

"Tell me about it."

What Chad Kenyon described was one of those nightmares that occur in many cities: He and his brother had recently bought a derelict, abandoned house on Webster Street. Since they'd moved with their usual speed and neglected to do their homework, they hadn't been aware that strange people were coming and going at all hours, displaying open hostility toward the neighbors. Teenagers and even younger children had been sneaking in, jeopardizing — so their parents claimed — life and limb. Household pets steered clear of the place, exercising animals' innate wisdom, which I wish we humans could tap into. The police came, the police went — the lack of a solution wasn't their fault. They were hamstrung by an overburdened department and city bureaucracy and an increasing crime rate.

It happens everywhere. Urban blight, they call it.

When he'd finished, I said, "I assume you came to us because you want the building cleared and secured."

"Right."

"And then what?"

"Well, I don't know. I've had one lowball offer on it — from a young girl named Michelle Curley — but I turned it down. She mentioned you, sort of as a character reference. Another reason I decided to talk with you personally. The kid's been pestering me. Maybe you can call her off."

Michelle and her family had been my neighbors on Church Street, and she'd done triple duty as my house and pet sitter, my chauffeur when the aftereffects of locked-in syndrome had legally prohibited me from propelling any kind of vehicle, and once — unknown to her mother — my co-investigator. She was now twenty-three, beautiful but with an offhand style that said she didn't dwell on her appearance, and determined to launch the biggest venture of her young life.

"I'll try to get her to stop bothering you. But I can't guarantee anything; she's headstrong."

"Yeah, she is. Well, anyway, if the house could be secured, maybe I could do some kind of rehab on it. It's a nice old place and I'm looking to set up a home. I'm tired of living in apartments and condos."

"Then let me tell you what this firm can and can't do in your case. We have to act legally, follow all state and local ordinances. Any illegal activity such as intimidating neighbors, even trespassers, would bring the Department of Consumer Affairs down on us, and if a case were proven against us, we'd lose our agency's license — forever. Now, there are strictly legal methods we can employ, but I'm afraid they'll be expensive."

"What kind of methods?"

"Extensive surveillance. Exterior photography, night and day. Infiltration by our operatives. Interior photography. Web cams. Utilizing our contacts within the SFPD, so they can make an early response to any trouble. Identification of the people entering and leaving the building, and thorough background checks on them. And that's not all — the list goes on and on. Are you sure you want to pursue this?"

"How expensive would it be?"

I calculated, then wrote down the figure on a note pad and passed it to him.

"That's a lot. Is there any cheaper stuff you can do?"

"We can look over the property, talk with the neighbors, do limited roll-by and walk-around surveillances. Neighbors are a particularly good source: someone always knows what's going on in any given place. We'll also keep in touch with our contacts at the SFPD and other city agencies. That kind of investigation would cost you less than half the more extensive job. And then, if we go forward, we won't add a surcharge."

He folded the paper and tucked it into his breast pocket. "Let's start with this then."

It was my kind of case. For all my negative feelings about the directions in which the city was going — extreme gentrification and the high housing costs that went with it; a transportation system that ran badly, if it ran at all; the NIMBYs and the homeless; the lack of important city services — it was still *my* city. If I could help reverse even one of those things, I'd give it a good shot.

I buzzed Ted and he entered with copies of the standard agency contract. Kenyon signed them and wrote out a personal check for the retainer it requested.

As he stood up to leave, he asked, "Sweetheart's not back, huh?"

"Not yet. I'll give her your regards."

"Thanks." Chad took the two remaining pizzettas from the tray and exited my office.

2:01 p.m.
I decided to take a run by the Webster Street house on my way to San José for my appointment with Gil Stratton, Renshaw's former employer at Quick Stops. Before I

49

left for San José I stopped by Mick's office. Earlier I'd asked him to take a break from Renshaw and scare up some information on the Webster Street house.

"About this new case," he said. "I'm coming up with all kinds of interesting stuff on the house. I can pull it together by this evening and e-mail it to you, or better yet, bring it by your place if you're going to be home."

Mick loves to be personally involved in my cases, and he wishes I'd allow him more time in the field, but — for now, at least — I needed him in the office directing our research. I couldn't deny him this chance to report his findings in his often dramatic style.

"Please come by. We'll be up late, as usual."

Then I headed for Webster Street.

The house was large, the color of its original paint unrecognizable beneath layers of grime and soot. A chain-link fence topped with barbed wire surrounded the lot, but here and there it had been breached. Graffiti dotted the house's walls, and most of the windows were broken. The small front yard was crammed with gasoline drums, old car parts, a threadbare couch, and other detritus.

As I set the alarm on my Mercedes, I thought of my beloved BMW Z4, burned to a crisp in my house fire two years ago. I hadn't liked any of the new BMWs, so Hy had given me the Mercedes SLK 350 roadster. Red, because it was my favorite color for cars, with a removable hardtop and black ragtop. One of the older models — which are much prettier than what they're making now — and extremely well maintained by its previous owner.

A strange choice to give an investigator who tried to stay in the background, but we both knew my days of going unrecognized were over. I'd received too much press, too much public exposure. Now I mostly let my operatives do the fieldwork, while I handled the more cerebral aspects of our cases. And frankly, I didn't miss sitting in a car for hours, my eyes aching with strain, bereft of good food, water, or a place to pee.

When I'd expressed my concern about taking the SLK into the bad neighborhoods I sometimes have to frequent, Hy had insisted no one would tamper with it; they'd probably think it belonged to a drug dealer. So far he'd been proven correct. Besides, it had one hell of an alarm that would blast the eardrums of anyone within a mile or more.

The reviews on this area, called the Western Addition, are mixed: many think it's dangerous, citing drive-by shootings that smack of gang warfare. Others love it for the relatively low rents and friendliness. Some cite the high crime rate, but actually it is about half that of many other areas of the city. True, there are housing projects, but they're slowly being upgraded — even the one nicknamed OC, for "out of control."

The block I was headed for was typical of the area: an eclectic mix of Victorians, more modern single-family homes, apartment buildings, and shops. Once the street was considered undesirable because of the old Central Freeway looming overhead, traffic noise resounding and fumes spewing day and night. But since the Loma Prieta quake of 1989 brought down the span, and with the spiking of real estate prices during the tech boom, the neighborhood's become a reasonably desirable place.

I found a parking space close to the southeast corner of the block. While small, most of the buildings were in decent enough condition, but others had been neglected and some were boarded up. And in the middle to the west was the source of blight that had poisoned the neighborhood. Even with watery fall sunlight peeking through wisps of fog, it looked poisonous.

As I crossed the street, I saw that the derelict house was in an even more shabby condition than it had seemed to be in from a distance: Cornices had broken off and were smashed in the small front yard. Redwood siding had been stripped.

Urban blight, at its worst. Why on earth had the Kenyons bought it?

As I mounted the front steps I clutched at the railing, avoiding missing boards. Inside, the air was bad — a mixture of mildew and decay and other odors I didn't even want to guess at. Heaps of old clothing and fabric decorated nearly every corner. The indoor light was dim but I couldn't make out many smeared footprints in the dust.

I pushed a light switch — one of the old two-button type. Nothing happened. The house probably hadn't been on the power grid for years.

The rooms were arranged in typical fashion for a Queen Anne Victorian: living room and library to either side of the front door; stairway ascending to the second story; spacious dining room with a fireplace to the left; large kitchen opposite. There was no furniture in the kitchen, just an antiquated iron stove and a stained porcelain sink. I tried the water taps but, as I'd expected, they didn't work. The enormous rat that skittered behind the stove appeared to be the only occupant at present.

I climbed the stairs to the second floor; they were sturdy, hardly giving beneath my weight. An example of the craftsmanship that had gone into these early dwellings. There were four empty bedrooms; in a fifth were a bare mattress and an empty jug of Gallo wine. A pair of men's Levi's, size thirty-six, and a red flannel shirt had been discarded on the floor. The room gave me the feeling that whoever had been squatting there had been gone for a long time. In a bathroom there was a claw-footed tub, an old-fashioned toilet with the water tank overhead, and a pedestal sink, broken and lying on its side. The tub had become a repository for broken ceramics, metal parts, and cardboard boxes and books and clothing that looked as if they had been gnawed at or perhaps infiltrated by worms. A couple of badly scarred window slats crowned the mess, from which a gamy odor arose. I didn't bother to investigate its source.

I went back to the stairway. Stopped, looking up at a large water stain on the ceiling. A scuffling noise came from behind me. Before I could turn, a hand landed hard between my shoulder blades. I tried to grasp the banister, fell, and tumbled down the stairs.

3:09 p.m.

After my head cleared somewhat, I looked at my watch, then lay very still, inventorying my pains and hoping I hadn't broken any bones. The back of my head hurt, as well as my shoulders and upper arms, but not seriously enough to indicate I had sustained a concussion or fractures. My vision was clear. I remained where I was, though, questions crowding my mind: Who had pushed me? Why? What did my attacker want? Had he been in the house for a long time? And if not, how had he entered the house without my seeing him?

The first answer: could have been anyone. A derelict who resented my intrusion was the most likely. Why? Same answer: someone didn't want me in what they considered their space. What did he want? To intimidate me, drive me away. How did he get inside? Vaguely I remembered a rear entrance to the kitchen, off an alley that would be shadowed even during the daylight hours. My attacker could have approached and slipped inside without my seeing him. Or he could've been inside the house the whole time. Why was I thinking in terms of "he" and not "she"? Because he'd pushed me high up on my back, arm angling. He was taller than most women — or men, for that matter.

Footsteps scurrying nearby. I tensed.

"Ma'am? Are you okay?"

The voice was childlike, and the hand that touched my forehead was small.

"I . . . don't . . . know." It hurt to open my eyes, and when I did, the freckled face of a boy, maybe ten years old, swam through the gloom.

"I'll go get my mom. She can help you." He scrambled away.

Another kid voice spoke. "We just came in and you were laying here at the bottom of the stairs."

My senses were slowly wakening from the shock — along with pain. I could already feel bumps and bruises forming. Experimentally I moved my head, then my arms and legs. "I don't think I broke anything. You see who pushed me?"

"No, ma'am, we didn't see nobody but you."

The kid, about the same age as the other one, was looking down at me now. His hair was carroty red and fell into long bangs over his eyes. He reminded me of the sons of my operative Patrick Neilan.

I pushed up into a sitting position. My left shoulder hurt like hell but previous experience told me a few aspirin would fix it up. "You play in this place?" I asked the kid.

"Yeah, sometimes. A lot of us do — not usually at night, though. At night there's grown-ups in here and they're kinda scary. Me and my brother heard you fall — otherwise we wouldn't've come in at all."

"You see anybody leaving?"

He shook his head, bangs flopping from side to side.

"These grown-ups," I asked, "how are they scary?"

"Mean-looking. Scruffy. They sit on the front steps and smoke dope and drink and do other drugs. Some of them try to get us to come up there, other guys call out obscene stuff to us, but most of them're too stoned to bother. One night we heard what my dad said were shots; he wanted to call the cops, but Mom said no. She's afraid the guys who hang there might figure out who called and come after us."

"Are there any women who hang here?"

"Some. Biker-type chicks with lots of tattoos. And then there were a couple of guys who were different."

"How do you mean, different?"

57

"Better dressed."

"Were they together?"

"No, they came at different times."

"When?"

"I dunno. Off and on in the last two weeks, anyway. We thought they might be from the city or real estate guys, but nothing's happened."

Hurried footsteps outside. A young woman pushed the boy aside and knelt beside me, shining a flashlight on my face. She had spiky blond hair, multiple piercings, and a kind face that looked down at me in concern. She said to the boys, "You two — home."

When they hesitated she added, "Now!" After they scooted out she asked me, "What happened here?"

I didn't want to make the neighbors any more uneasy about the house than they already were. "I slipped on the stairs, but I'm okay," I said. "Just shaken up."

She lifted my wrist. "I took a CPR course," she added after a minute. "Your pulse rate's real high. Maybe you should go to the ER."

I thought of all the times I'd been confined to hospitals, the long stays when I'd had locked-in syndrome. "I don't need the ER."

She shrugged. "Okay, if you say so. What were you doing here?"

"My firm is trying to clear up the problem of this attractive nuisance. I'm glad your boys found me; I might've lain here for hours."

She looked around, shivered. "I wouldn't want to lie here for two *minutes*. Those of us who live nearby have come to hate the place. It's not so much that we're worried about our property values — not in this city — but our kids . . . we forbid them to come in here, but you know how kids are. You ready to stand up?"

"I'm fine now."

She assisted me to my feet — expertly and gently.

I said, "That CPR class must've been really good. And I suspect you have a natural talent for helping people."

Even in the dim light, I could see her face flush with pleasure. "Thanks. I'm starting nurse's training at SF State next term."

She helped me out of the house. When we reached the sidewalk, I pointed out my car, and she whistled. "Too cool! Maybe someday my husband and I'll be able to afford one like it. But by the time that happens, the boys'll be old enough to take it out and wreck it."

I switched off the alarm. As I eased into the driver's seat, I said, "Hey, I don't even know your name."

"Emily Parsons."

"Sharon McCone." I handed her my card, and we shook hands through the lowered window.

"A private investigator," she said. "Well, you sure picked some house to investigate."

"How long have you lived in the neighborhood?"

"I was raised here in the house where we live now, but after high school I went to college at USC, got married, and we lived in the Valley until five years ago, when my dad died. My husband requested a transfer to his company's office up here so we could take care of Mom, and we moved in with her."

"Has your mother mentioned anybody who occupied this house during the time you lived down south?"

"I think she said there was a family who were going to move in a number of years back." She furrowed her brow. "I can't remember their name, though. She has a picture of them, I think. Mom and Dad had been on vacation in Arizona, and there were a couple of frames left on the film — that was before digital was common — so Mom offered to photograph them on the steps of their new home. It must be in the boxes of pictures she always plans to put in albums and then doesn't."

"Could you try to find it for me? It could be important to my case."

"Sure. Maybe it'll nudge Mom into getting the family album project going."

"Thanks. And if there's anything I can do for you or the boys —" I started.

She smiled shyly. "Nothing for me, but the boys might like some chocolate."

"I used to be a chocoholic. What kind?"

"Ghirardelli — local loyalty, of course. Dark — it's healthier."

"You've got a deal." I gave her money for the candy, then watched her walk back to her house. A couple of times she shot me concerned glances over her shoulder.

A good, caring woman, I thought. She'd probably make an excellent nurse.

I sat at the curb till I felt okay to drive. Reflected again upon who had pushed me down those stairs. Gage Renshaw entered my mind, but I dismissed him; sneak attacks just weren't his style. Or were they? I knew so little about the man he'd become. Really didn't know much about the man he'd been. But how could Renshaw have known I was going to be at Webster Street alone? How could he even have known about Webster Street? No, the person was a stranger. Had to be.

4:19 p.m.
I phoned and rescheduled my appointment with Gil Stratton for the next day, then headed back to the office. Mick recognized my step as I started past his bailiwick and waved me in.

"There's nothing new on Renshaw and his whereabouts," he said. "But Hank called; he researched some additional case law, and he's sure we don't have any legal problems regarding ownership of the agency. And I've got some background on the Webster Street house." He swiveled around, saw I was still standing, and said, "Sit."

"Maybe you and Alison ought to get yourselves a dog."

He looked at me, frowning. "A dog?"

"Well, you seem good at giving commands like you would to a puppy."

"You okay?"

"Lousy day." I sat down gingerly on Derek's desk chair.

"What happened to you? You're moving kind of funny."

"Long story," I said, and proceeded to tell him.

"You've *really* had a bad day," he said

when I'd finished. "Maybe you should go home and rest. We can go over this info tomorrow."

"Best opinion I've heard yet."

■ ■ ■ ■

WEDNESDAY, OCTOBER 7

■ ■ ■ ■

1:30 p.m.

As freeways go, the Bay Shore is one of the oldest in Northern California, dating from the 1920s. In the forties and fifties it was nicknamed the Bloody Bay Shore because of the number of spectacular and often fatal accidents that occurred on its lanes. Now it's safer — probably because people are more used to freeways — but it's still ugly, running through light industrial areas and past SFO, and fronted by dreary apartment complexes and subdivisions. Today much of it is surrounded by sound walls between which the traffic roars and the air is oppressive. It becomes more oppressive as you near San José, a megalopolis that seems to be competing with LA for the title of smog capital of California.

Mineta San José International used to be a small outlying field with few movements — the aviation term for landings and takeoffs — but with the explosion of tech industries in Silicon Valley, it now almost rivals SFO for traffic. Quick Stops, the FBO Gage Renshaw had once flown for, was located on Aviation Avenue, not far from the field.

I supposed I could have flown down, but at the time I'd left it had seemed a great deal of effort to drive to Oakland Airport's North Field, where Hy and I kept our Cessna 170B, preflight, and probably refuel. (I couldn't remember how full the tanks had been when we last flew.) Besides, what I found out from Stratton might have required me to go on to a place where there was no decent airstrip or ground transportation.

Quick Stops' building was a corrugated iron shed that had seen better days. I parked and entered. It contained one room with a couple of cluttered desks and a row of file cabinets. A bespectacled, bald-headed man bent over the larger desk riffling through files. "Where is that goddamn invoice?" he muttered to himself. Without looking up at me, he said, "Gina, get your ass over here and find the AV gas invoice for last month — they called and said it's overdue."

I shut the door behind me. "I'm not Gina."

He raised his eyes. "Oh, shit! You're not. I'm sorry."

"People have told me to do worse things than locate an invoice." I introduced myself and presented my card, and his confusion vanished.

"That's right. We made an appointment. I'm Gil Stratton."

We shook hands.

"Sit down, please. If I know Gina, she's over in the shop, flirting with the mechanics." He removed a stack of flight manuals from a chair and put them on the smaller desk; they immediately fell on the floor. Stratton threw up his hands and gave me a what-can-you-do look.

When we were seated, he said, "On the phone you told Gina you want to talk about Gage Renshaw. It's a name I haven't heard in quite a while. What's he been doing?"

I explained that he had stayed on in Asia and flown for K-Air for a while along with my business partner, Hy Ripinsky. That he'd then teamed up with Dan Kessell, owner of K-Air, and they'd returned stateside. That for a few years the two of them operated an executive protection service called Renshaw & Kessell International, and were later occasionally joined by Hy, in the capacity of a troubleshooter. And that shortly after, Dan

Kessell was murdered and Renshaw disappeared.

"Who killed Kessell?" Stratton asked. "Renshaw, maybe?"

Same suspicion I harbored. "It's possible. The file's still open."

"And what happened to their company?"

"Ripinsky took it over, operating it on a strictly legal basis — which often wasn't the case before. A year ago, give or take a few months, he and I merged our respective firms into McCone & Ripinsky International. But now Renshaw's reappeared and refuses to tell us what he wants from us."

"You and Ripinsky fifty-fifty partners?"

"I should say so. We're also husband and wife."

"Jesus! Never thought any woman could tame the Old Rip down."

"Actually, I'm his second wife. I can credit his first for doing a lot of the taming."

"What happened to her?"

"She died."

"Sorry to hear that. How?"

"Not violently, if that's what you're thinking. She had MS."

"Tough break for both of them."

Julie Spaulding had been a woman I was sure I would have liked: an environmental activist, in spite of the fact that she'd been

70

confined to a wheelchair since her teens; a writer who hadn't been afraid to publish her sometimes inflammatory opinions in letters to the editors of many newspapers and magazines; an advisor to various fledgling ecologically oriented associations. And she actually hadn't tamed Hy; in fact, she'd given him a good bit of rope, just not enough to hang himself with. It was only after her death that he went wild — taking crazy risks and allying himself with the extreme element of the environmental movement. Before I first met him, a friend had told me he'd settled down but was "still dangerous." The characterization applies to him to this very day — and the years have proven that a good deal of that dangerous quality has rubbed off on me.

I changed the subject back to business and explained to Stratton about Renshaw's possible designs on McCone & Ripinsky.

Stratton thought for a moment. "Seems like a problem for a lawyer."

"We've got one working on it."

"Then why come to me?"

"I'm hoping that you can give me some insight into Renshaw's character."

"Hmmm." Stratton pushed back from his desk and put his feet up on top. His loafers were new Guccis, their soles barely scuffed.

The FBO business must be picking up, along with the rest of the economy.

At length he said, "I don't think Gage has much character. At least not in the way we usually think of it. If anything, he's socio-pathic. Gage is the center of his universe, surrounded by people who, in his eyes, might as well be cardboard cutouts. Some-times he gets off on torturing his cutouts — which is what he's currently doing to you and Ripinsky."

"He *tortures* people?"

"Not in the conventional sense. But emo-tionally and mentally he enjoys putting the screws on. When he worked for me he especially liked to scare the clients who weren't familiar or comfortable with flying. Made rough passes at unaccompanied women. Two customers reported us to the Better Business folks. That was it for Gage and me; I cut him his final check and showed him the door."

"You have any idea of where he went after that?"

"No, ma'am. I didn't care, so long as he left me alone. I called him a sociopath before, but now that I think about him, I revise my opinion. I'd say he's borderline psychotic."

"You sound like a psychologist."

"Master's from San José State. I was going to go on for the PhD, but I found out I was better with airplanes than other people's neuroses." His gaze moved away from me, looking into the past.

"Do you know anyone in the Bay Area Renshaw may have contacted?"

"A couple of folks have mentioned seeing him recently in dive bars downtown. They said he looked like he was on the skids, gave him a wide berth."

"Did they tell you which bars?"

"One was the Front. The other I don't recall."

"Are you willing to give me the people's names?"

"Sorry, I'm not. They're good customers."

"And there's nobody else Renshaw might've been in touch with?"

Stratton paused thoughtfully. "I've never known Gage to have a friend, or even a lover. As I said before, we're all cardboard figures to him. People like him can't make friends."

5:13 p.m.

On the way to the freeway, I drove past the Front, the dive bar Stratton had named. It was closed — permanently — with slabs of plywood over its door. No way of finding

73

out if anybody who worked there or frequented it could help me locate Renshaw.

So where do you go in a big metropolitan area when you have no friends?

Scruffy-looking Renshaw, with that white streak in his hair and his jutting features, would stand out in even the busiest hotel or motel clerk's mind. I called Mick and he confirmed that no one his operatives had questioned had recalled such an individual registering, or recognized Renshaw's photograph, which Mick had gotten off the tapes from our surveillance cams. There was no paper trail either: apparently Renshaw had no credit cards or, if he did, he wasn't using them. He could have used bogus or stolen cards, but that would have entailed his keeping on the move as the frauds or thefts were reported. From what I knew of the man, I sensed he would prefer to carry out his scams from a fixed — and probably comfortable — location.

So where, dammit, was that location? Where *was* he?

His reappearance was already sucking up all my energy —

Of course! I realized. That was exactly what he wanted to do. Distract, confuse, and then strike. Do the unexpected, and then sit back and gloat. Profit when the moment was right.

But distract me from *what?* I reviewed the cases we had on our plate, but none of them seemed important enough to prompt a con man of Renshaw's style to come out of hiding after so many years.

Or *had* he been hiding after all? He was a careless man, slipping away without a word, never contacting anyone until it suited some whim or other. But he was also a purposeful man when he wanted to be, and what I feared was that purpose.

6:01 p.m.
Naturally I got trapped in early rush-hour traffic. Moving along inch by inch through Peninsula towns such as San Carlos, San Mateo, Millbrae, and San Bruno, I tried to amuse myself by imagining the lives of the people who lived there, but all I came up with was trite and out-of-date versions of the lifestyles depicted in old films. Truth was, movies like *No Down Payment* were my reference point, and they didn't reflect modern suburban reality.

Lord knew I hadn't been raised in such an environment. Our old, rambling house on one of San Diego's finger canyons had been like few others. Plants had grown lushly — many of them vegetables in the

75

filled-in swimming pool that a sonic boom from nearby NAS Miramar had irreparably cracked. Birds, which my mother loved, had flown freely in and out of the house. (I learned the ability to duck my head fast, because I was deathly afraid of birds, bats, and other airborne things. It was a wonder I'd ever become a pilot, much less married one.)

As for the rest of us — well, we'd flown away like Ma's birds eventually did. Years ago my eldest — and now only — brother John had bought the house from the rest of us and raised two terrific boys there. Sometimes he made noises about selling it, but I hoped he wouldn't; it's nice to know you've got a homeplace to return to.

7:10 p.m.

My new homeplace — a single-family Spanish-style house on Avila Street in the Marina district, only a few blocks from the Bayside Green — was a joy to return to. When I'd first seen it, I couldn't believe anyone would give it up — much less that we could afford it. But the owner had died, and the heirs lived in Florida. They wanted it off their hands quickly and priced it to sell.

We'd toured it the first day it came on the

76

market. The Spanish style had always appealed to us, and the red-nosed garden gnome — which we named Adolphus after Hy's uncle and only living relative — was a nice finishing touch. Somebody had slipped a bid in before us, but that deal fell through, and only six weeks later we found ourselves under our new roof and inundated with new stuff.

Since virtually all our possessions had been destroyed when our earthquake house on Church Street succumbed to a vicious arsonist, we needed everything, and we indulged ourselves in a fit of crass consumerism that nauseates me to this very day. I console myself with the fact that it was the insurance company's money — and they'd been bleeding us dry for years — but still, we could have exercised *some* restraint.

In a matter of weeks we'd acquired soft, buttery leather chairs and sofas. A Sleep Number bed and comfy linens and big towels. Large flat-screen wall-mounted TVs. Dining room set. Area rugs. Pots, pans, flatware, and dishes. Flowers for the garden and outdoor furniture for the deck. Antique rolltop desk. The list went on and on. . . .

I doubted we could stuff another thing into the place.

Clothing purchases were fun: for me, jeans

and sweaters and jackets and shoes from such outlets as Lands' End; for Hy, pretty much the same. I made a trip to pick up a quality black business suit and a semiformal dress from one of the downtown department stores; Hy drove to our place at the coast and brought back some extra things we kept there. No reason to fetch anything from the ranch near Tufa Lake: if you appeared there in garments more elegant than faded jeans and flannel, they'd probably have you locked up as a public nuisance.

But our buying frenzy had ended now, and we both admitted we felt purged of the compulsion. To make up for it we were prepared to give back — or forward, whatever the current term was. We'd funded a small foundation to grant aviation scholarships and soon would begin evaluating applications. Those accepted would receive tuition and expenses to a number of high-quality flight schools across the nation. And a chance to take to the skies like us, the fearless flyers who kept crashing into things like mountains.

9:15 p.m.

Mick had called to tell me when he'd be by with the information on the Webster Street house and, as usual, he was punctual. I don't know how he does it — some extremely accurate inner clock, no doubt — but he must've gotten the gene from his father's side of the family. No one in my family has ever been punctual, except for food-and-booze-laden wakes after a funeral.

Hy and I had spent an anxious evening, eating tacos (a joint effort; I fry the tortillas while he makes the filling) and watching reruns of old series on TV, trying to pretend Renshaw's sudden appearance wouldn't turn out to be ruinous. A cable channel was airing episodes of *The Avengers,* and each time Diana Rigg — in her Emma Peel suit — overcame a villain, I mentally praised and envied her prowess. But at about nine, I dozed off, my head on Hy's shoulder.

Enter Mick.

Hy made coffee while I tried to wake up and collect my wits. Then we settled around the kitchen table.

Mick said, "There's a lot of background on that house on Webster Street. Was built in 1890 by William Acton, one of the minor silver-mine barons. Four of his six children were wiped out in the smallpox epidemic of 1887; two others died of pneumonia in the early 1900s. His wife Louise then proceeded to lose her mind and became one of those crazy-lady-in-the-attic cases until her death in 1935."

"Cause of death?"

"Suicide. She threw herself out the attic window. William Acton survived, however, well into his nineties."

"Alone in that house?"

"Except for a housekeeper, Susan Whitby, whom he later married. They had two daughters — Phylippa, born in 1944, and Chrysanthus, born in 1952."

"What happened to them?"

Mick consulted his notes. "Phylippa Acton never married and died in 2009 in that ritzy retirement home down near the bridge — you know where I mean."

I did. The city is full of landmarks, wherever you habitually travel, and this one was close to Avila Street.

"And the other sister?"

"That's where the thread of the timeline breaks. No record. Chrysanthus was eight years younger than her sister, so it's possible she's still alive."

"Phylippa and Chrysanthus. The Acton family must've been heavy into the Greek."

"Their last name's Americanized from Akakios."

"I see. Other details on either daughter?"

"Phylippa was born in the city on April 4, 1944. Attended rich people's schools here and in Marin. After that she did nothing."

"Nothing?"

"Nope. Seems it was deemed proper for ladies of her station and era to be decorative and entertaining — until marriage, of course."

"Did she marry?"

"No. There were suitors, but the war interfered."

"And Chrysanthus?"

"She married a Nathan Smithson, and had a son, Adam Smithson, but the trail ends there. No record of Chrysanthus or her husband and son beyond the late eighties."

"Did Acton have any other children with his second wife?"

"No."

"Who inherited the house?"

"Both sisters. Their mother predeceased Acton by a year. The attorney for the estate conducted a thorough search for the Smithsons or any other living relative when Phylippa died, but came up empty-handed."

"So the estate maintained the house?"

"Right. It paid all bills and property taxes. It's only in the past several years that they allowed it to go to hell."

"Why, do you suppose?"

"Maybe the estate couldn't afford the

costs — which would be considerable. That might be why they sold out to the Kenyons."

"Who was executor of the estate?"

"Wells Fargo bank and, no, I don't have any contacts there, but Thelia does, and she's trying to get at their records."

Mick had practically invented the term *hacker.*

I said, "You'll manage."

■ ■ ■ ■

THURSDAY, OCTOBER 8

■ ■ ■ ■

11:11 a.m.

As soon as Ted could arrange it, I held a staff meeting to brief everyone on the threat posed to us by Gage Renshaw. Each received the photo of him and a background sheet.

Then while they all went about their various assignments, I sat in my office, as usual chafing at the paperwork that had appeared in my in-boxes, both physically and on the computer screen.

I was saved from drudgery by the phone buzzing. Ted. "I've got Inspector Larry Kaufman on line one for you."

I'd left a message for Larry at his office at the SFPD earlier. Kaufman specialized in undercover relations and was a damn good cop. In the years I'd known him, he'd turned around many a potentially explosive situation with his steady-handedness, tact, and humor.

"Thanks." I switched over to Kaufman.

"McCone, I hear gloom in your voice," he said. "That referral I sent you last month, did it go bad?"

"No. I'm sorry I haven't thanked you for it earlier. But I'm calling about a personal problem." I laid the Renshaw situation out for him.

When I finished, he said, "This is a tough one, in terms of the law. Renshaw may have bilked half of South America, but you say he hasn't pulled off anything here."

"That we know of."

"And that ties my hands — at least officially. Unofficially I can put an officer on him part time, but if he spots him or her, it'll tip him to the fact we're interested in him."

"I think Gage always assumes people are interested in him."

"Egomaniac, huh? Okay, I'll have somebody look into where he's staying."

"Great. Thank you."

Larry sighed heavily. "Are you sure you don't know of any crimes — preferably the kind where statutes of limitations haven't run out — that this Renshaw has committed on American soil?"

"No, but I've got a researcher working on that."

"Well, we'll keep each other posted."

2:07 p.m.

I set up a schedule for two of my newest hires for surveilling the Webster Street property, then checked with Mick and his department on the results of their search for Renshaw's whereabouts. No luck so far, but as soon as I came back from a late lunch at one of the food trucks that prowled downtown — a hot dog on a pretzel bun — Renshaw called "to chat."

"I have nothing to 'chat' with you about," I said as I hit the button to record the conversation.

"Sharon, stop being so defensive."

"Look, you! You've done many dreadful things in your life. When you disappeared, we were relieved that you were gone. No — we hoped you were dead. And now it turns out you were in parts of South America during that time."

"Sharp as ever with your research, aren't you?"

"Yes, I'm sharp, and I have an even sharper tech staff. They'll find out what you want from us eventually, but I hate to waste the man power, so why don't you just tell me?"

"Why would I want to do that? It'll be fun to watch McCone and Ripinsky squirm."

"Maybe we should sit down and talk this

thing through. Where're you staying?"

"Uh-uh, McCone."

"Then come here to the offices."

"Not to your home? That lovely Spanish-style house on Avila Street?"

That's right — he knows exactly where we live.

"We separate our business lives from our private lives."

"Yeah. That's why two members of your staff had dinner with you at your house last Saturday."

Adah Joslyn and Craig Morland were both our operatives, but close friends as well. She, a former SFPD homicide inspector, and he, a former special agent of the FBI, had met during one of my cases and enjoyed a whirlwind courtship that had ended in Craig's leaving the Bureau and Washington, D.C., far behind him. They'd eventually married, and so far their working relationship seemed as compatible as their personal one. It was not unusual for them to have dinner at our house.

I said, "Have you been spying on us, Renshaw? Spying on our friends and associates?"

"What do you think?"

"I think you're a sneaky bastard."

He laughed. "That's me, all right. And

88

thorough, like you. I also know that your nephew and his lady have a nice house on Potrero Hill. And that Hank Zahn and the Altman broad are still at the same place; their daughter's grown up into a real pretty young woman."

At the mention of Hank and Anne-Marie's adopted daughter, my blood pressure spiked. Renshaw had reportedly enticed a young Venezuelan girl to steal from her family and run off with him; what might he do to Habiba? "Don't you dare to go near her, Renshaw. Don't you *dare!*"

"You know the effect I have on young women, maybe even older women like yourself."

I couldn't go on with this call. He was toying with my emotions. I started to speak, but I knew my voice would give away how enraged and upset I was, so instead I hung up on him.

Renshaw didn't call back.

2:33 p.m.

I arranged a conference call with Hank and Anne-Marie to warn them about Renshaw and the possible threat to Habiba. Of the two of them, she took the news far more calmly.

"Are you sure this isn't just idle talk

designed to scare you?" she asked.

"Could be, but with someone like Renshaw, it's best to be aware, take precautions."

"Well, she's already a cautious kid, considering what she's been through." Habiba's childhood had been chaotic, and extricating her from that chaos had involved a great deal of danger. If anyone knew the warning signs of danger, it was she.

"She's got to be told," Hank said.

"Of course," Anne-Marie agreed.

"And perhaps removed from harm's way," I added. "Is there anyplace the three of you could go until we get Renshaw in hand?"

"Well, Hank and I certainly can't leave our clients up in the air, and she has school, but maybe Helene . . ."

"Who's that?"

"Helene Herber, the headmistress of her school. She and Habiba are very fond of each other."

"A school administrator? I'm not sure —"

"This particular schoolmarm lives in a super-high-security building. And, although Hank and I don't approve, she's a card-carrying member of the NRA."

"A rabid member?" I myself opposed the NRA and their inflexible stance on gun control, especially as it applied to semiautomatic weapons.

Anne-Marie chuckled. "Helene's no gun nut. In fact, she's been censured by the local chapter for speaking out on the need for caution in gun ownership and for assessing what appears to be a threatening situation before you blast away. If you want, I'll call her and ask if she can take Habiba in. It shouldn't be a problem. But shouldn't the two of you be taking precautions also?"

"Don't worry about us." Like Habiba's headmistress, we didn't adhere to the shoot-first-and-think-later approach to firearms, but we each owned weapons and knew how to use them. Hy liked them better than I, having grown up in the rough-and-ready high desert country, but my old .38 Special had saved my life more than once. It, and maybe even my .45, which I seldom carried, would have to come out of their secure storage places till Renshaw was dealt with.

My appointments and conferences with various staff members done for the day, I decided it was time to check out how the surveillance was going on the derelict house on Webster Street.

4:21 p.m.
I came face-to-face with my operative Roberta Cruz on the sidewalk in front of

the house. She was tall, nearly six feet, with bluntly cut black hair and an elongated face that looked homely until she smiled. When she did, her wide mouth and sparkling dark eyes could light up a room. Today she was in a solemn mood.

"How's the surveillance going?" I asked.

"I did a couple of drive-bys, then walked around and checked out the neighborhood and the property. There're multiple ways into the house: front door, back door, broken windows on all floors. Even a hole in the roof that a mountain climber might use if he or she was so inclined. A redheaded kid and a gaggle of other boys stopped and looked at it; from the kid's gestures, he seemed to be showing something off."

"Probably one of the Parsons boys from up the street. They found me when I was pushed down the stairs and went for their mother to help me."

Roberta crossed her arms, hands clutching her shoulders. "When I got here, I toured the inside. God, it's a depressing place. I can't believe kids actually want to play there. But I do understand why the derelicts like to hang out there at night." She glanced at her watch. "My relief isn't here yet, and I've got a date." She grinned gleefully. "Imagine that — a real date with a hetero male in San Francisco."

"You take off, Roberta. I'll relieve you till Courtney gets here."

She practically skipped down the block.

I could understand her elation: ours is not a city known for frequent or successful love connections — be they hetero, same-sex, or any of the other variations. I don't know why, but I'm a prime example: none of my relationships worked until I traveled to the high desert and nabbed Hy.

As it turned out, I had a while to wait for the arrival of the other operative I'd assigned to the surveillance, Courtney Masson. I have an ironclad rule that I explain to all new hires: three times you're late for an assignment, you're warned, four and you're fired. This was Courtney's number three, and she seemed oblivious to the time as she glided effortlessly along the sidewalk. Her blond hair was pulled into a ponytail, her makeup perfect, her sweater and slacks — probably cashmere — spotless and without a wrinkle. A few yards away, she stopped, took out a compact, and refreshed her lipstick — never bothering to glance at the target of her surveillance. When she saw me sitting outside the house on the steps, her hand flew to her mouth.

I said, "That's number three, Courtney."

"Sharon, oh, my God, I had an important phone call. My uncle in . . . Des Moines is seriously ill."

I doubted that she, or any members of her family, had ever been to Des Moines.

"Come sit next to me," I said, patting the step.

She did, first wiping off the step and adjusting her pants to avoid rumpling them. "Look, I'll make up the time."

"You're just playing at this job, aren't you?" I asked.

"I don't understand what you mean."

"Playing at being an investigator. It gives you a certain cachet. You probably tell stories about your exploits at parties. Overly exaggerated stories."

Her gaze flicked away from mine. I'd nailed her.

"The problem with that," I went on, "is that you don't know what being an investigator is all about. You don't understand or abide by the rules of confidentiality. And that's a very dangerous thing. And we cover one another's asses. What if you and I were in trouble? In the sights of a potential shooter's Glock? What would you do?"

"Run like hell, I suppose."

"Leaving me to do battle. And probably getting yourself shot in the back. Maybe get both of us killed."

"But things like that don't happen —"

"They happen all the time. Just read the newspapers."

"They don't happen to *me*!" Her voice escalated.

"No, they don't. And I certainly don't want them to. That's why I'm letting you go."

Shocked silence. "You're *firing* me?"

"Yes. I'm sorry, but it's best for the agency — and best for you."

She stood, shaking all over like a dog that's been doused with water. "You'll be hearing from my lawyer about this!"

"That's your right."

"You bitch!" The words echoed up and down the quiet street.

I just looked steadily at her. She turned and stormed up the block, turned a corner, and was gone.

Another problem. They come in batches. And I particularly don't like this one. Don't like this case either. Jesus, my last major case centered on a vacant lot owned by the Kenyon brothers and filled with cast-off crap. Now this!

9:32 p.m.

Hy and I were at a formal reception at The Academy of Sciences in Golden Gate Park

— an event we'd scheduled months ago and couldn't back out of — for Save the Animals of San Francisco, one of the many ecological organizations of which he was on the board. He was being his usual charming self and I was hating every moment of it.

Becoming more and more surly by the minute, truth be told. Twice I'd traveled down the escalator to view the fish, and twice I'd suffered the smothering, damp heat of the rain forest's exotic plants until I'd gotten to the observation deck on the third level, where I could cool off in the fresh air. A few times I'd stepped behind pillars or turned my head to avoid people I knew.

The Academy is now housed in a relatively new structure in Golden Gate Park, and the Steinhart Aquarium is one of its gems, containing a vast assortment of creatures, both marine and amphibious. The displays in which they are housed replicate their natural habitats and reflect the diversity of their environments. I especially love the Philippine Coral Reef Gallery — one of the largest displays of an undersea wonderland in the world. Sometimes I stand before it mesmerized, imagining myself dwelling inside — zipping through the formations, streamlined and supple and free. Tonight, though, the aquarium wasn't doing anything for me; even Claude, the rare albino alligator residing in the Swamp Gallery, failed to charm me.

Usually I'm pretty perky at parties and in crowds. If you grow up in a house where relatives and friends are always arriving without being invited and staying till they're given notice to vacate, you have to be. In college it had been much the same: long late-night conversations on the back stairs of an old house that an ever-changing ragtag collection of us had shared on Durant Avenue near the UC Berkeley campus.

But after graduation, when I'd discovered that a BA in sociology didn't mean much of anything in the real world, I'd returned to working the job that I'd held part time as an all-night security guard in a downtown San Francisco office building, and surprisingly found pleasure in the solitude. Even later when I was hired by All Souls Legal Cooperative, where one of the very few perks was living in its big Victorian, I'd sought out a small studio apartment not far away on Guerrero Street.

Alone, but not lonely. And why should I be?

I'd had relationships (mostly disastrous) and bought and renovated a cottage built as shelter for people made homeless by the earthquake of 1906, and if it hadn't been for an encounter with Hy while on a case in the high desert of Mono County, I might have been living in that manner still.

But Hy . . .

I smiled at the memory of our first encounter on the shores of Tufa Lake:

"Hey," I'd called, "what's your name?"

"Heino Ripinsky."

Jesus, I thought, *it's no wonder he didn't introduce himself earlier!*

Hy must have been used to reactions like mine, because he stopped beside his ancient Morgan, whirled, and leveled an index finger at me. "Don't laugh," he warned. "Don't you dare laugh!"

I controlled the twitching at the corners of my mouth and spread my hands wide. "Me? Why would I do that?"

He winked at me, vaulted into the Morgan, and was gone in a cloud of dust.

Now Hy touched my elbow — his signal that he wanted out of there.

In the elevator on the way down, he said, "God, those people have gotten stuffy! Ecologically oriented mutual funds. Shares in sustainable corporate farms. Getting in on the ground floor of safe genetically engineered foods. Makes me want to organize a protest and get involved in a fistfight."

Seemed that, in my isolation, I'd had a somewhat better time than Hy. I squeezed his arm in sympathy.

"You must be exhausted," he went on. "This stuff with Renshaw —"

"Must exhaust you too."

"Well, sure." The elevator stopped at the garage level and we turned toward our assigned spaces. "I just don't understand what he —"

"Let's give the subject a rest for a while."

"But aren't you worried —"

"As you said, I'm exhausted."

Understanding, he smiled as he held the door of my car open for me, then turned toward his own. "See you at home, Mc-Cone. First one who gets naked wins the prize."

"What prize?"

"Me."

"Oh, hell. I won that years ago."

11:10 p.m.

After I collected my prize, I couldn't sleep. Instead, as I often did, I lay in the dark and reflected on the years during Hy's and my time together. We'd had joy, adventures, conflicts, and near-disasters that had all bonded us closer. What would have blown other couples apart had only served to unite us. I wondered what was yet to come.

More and more I heard people somewhat older than I — not to say a fair number of my contemporaries — talking about retirement. The concept had begun to puzzle me.

What did it actually mean? I asked people. *Not having to get up and go to work in the morning.*

But once you get up, what do you do?

Relax, play some golf or maybe some bridge. Buy a good bike and ride everywhere. Plant a garden, take up that hobby you abandoned ten years ago, volunteer at the animal shelter or the library.

Sounded good, but I'd listened to a lot of such plans, and noticed they didn't often come to fruition. I never saw a familiar face in my visits to the animal shelter — where I *did* volunteer. No gardens bloomed in our former neighbors' yards; hardly any happy people went off carrying golf bags or other sports equipment, few bikes ridden by older people whizzed by. But what I did observe was a number of envious glances from previously friendly neighbors of a certain age being directed at me as I went about my busy day. In the new neighborhood, which had become something of a Mecca for families with children, I didn't notice that kind of resentment.

I understood and empathized with the reasons for the older people's resentment: life had tricked them in a nasty way. Promises of an easy, pleasurable old age had been broken by the failing economy, by the greedy corporations that had fueled the recent recession, by the politicians who didn't have the guts to stand up for the issues we'd elected them on.

The American dream had worked splendidly for the young and well educated who could command top earnings; and by sheer luck and hard work (and, frankly, a certain amount of chicanery on Hy's part) it had worked for us. But for many of the rest it had turned out not to be a dream after all. And in some cases it had become a nightmare.

■ ■ ■ ■

FRIDAY,
OCTOBER 9

■ ■ ■ ■

9:22 a.m.

I found a pleasant surprise when I arrived at my office in the morning: my young friend Michelle Curley.

"Hey, how's it going?" I asked, dumping files, briefcase, and purse on the desk.

"Pretty well." She reached forward and prevented the vase containing the deep-red rose that weekly appeared on my desk, courtesy of Hy, from toppling onto the floor. (Those roses — that's a whole other story.) When we were settled, she added, "I need to ask you a business — or maybe it's a legal — question."

"I'm not an expert in either of those areas. Maybe you should talk to Hank or Anne-Marie." When I saw her frown, I added, "They probably wouldn't charge you."

Michelle had passed on going to college and started her own firm, Natural Habitat Associates. So far as I knew, the only associates were her little brother, Sean, and whoever her current boyfriend might be. But I had great hopes for the fledgling company: Chelle — as she preferred to be called — had been buying, rehabilitating, and profitably reselling dilapidated houses since she was eighteen, aided by her parents, who cosigned loans and helped out whenever they could. Now, according to Chad Kenyon, she wanted to take on a major rehab job — on Webster Street.

She now said, "I think you're more suited to help me."

"Oh? Why?"

"There's this place I really want. It's shit now — not even habitable — but I've got a vision."

"I know. Chad Kenyon told me."

"He *did* come to see you."

"He also hired us to clear the building of squatters and other intruders. So we'd better not catch you on the premises."

Chelle frowned. "I thought maybe you could persuade the Kenyons to negotiate with me. But you seem so negative."

I asked, "You've been hanging around that dump, haven't you?"

"Sometimes."

"Sleeping there? You told me you do that, you know."

"Don't worry about me. I've got any problems covered."

"How?"

"You're about to meet him. He's waiting out front."

A boyfriend, then. That was a relief — somewhat.

A tall, good-looking man was soon admitted to the office by Ted. Blond, lightly bearded, he looked to be in his mid-thirties. A little old for Chelle, I thought.

She jumped up and went to take his hand. "Shar, meet Nemo James."

We shook hands and I motioned for them to sit. "Has Chelle taken you to the Webster Street house?" I asked.

"Sure. A few times."

"Are you aware it's dangerous?"

He shrugged. "I've got a gun for protection."

"He won't let me touch it," Chelle said.

"Good. What do you think of the place?"

"That it's a gold mine ready for the old pick and shovel."

"Are you by any chance from the West?"

"How'd you . . . ? Oh, the 'old pick and shovel' bit. Yeah, I'm from Utah."

"So," Chelle said, "are you willing to help me with the Kenyons, Shar?"

"I'll try, but that's all I can promise."

"I knew you would!"

"Don't get your hopes up yet," I told her.

10:21 a.m.

It still struck me as a bad idea for Chelle to rehab the Webster Street house. A very bad idea for a variety of reasons. The tough dealing Kenyons were one factor in the mix; the squatters who would infringe on Chelle's efforts were another. The job would be crushingly expensive and at best she'd turn only a small profit. The place was depressing and, if she and Nemo decided to live there while doing much of the work, as she often did with her dilapidated buildings, it would surely put a strain on their relationship. But the danger of such an endeavor bothered me most. A push down the stairs by an unknown assailant was bad enough; what would happen if matters turned lethal?

I should have told Chelle and Nemo about my fears, but they seemed determined to pursue their plans. I hoped the Kenyons would continue to refuse to sell.

Again, it was one of those complications of life that I didn't need, given the others. So I merely asked her for a prospectus on her project and told her I'd be in touch. Then, when I was sure they'd cleared the elevator doors, I pounded my fists on the

108

desk and shouted, "Ripinsky!"

He came running. "What the hell's going on?"

"My life's turning into a nightmare!"

"You mean Renshaw? I can handle him."

"Please do — brutally, if necessary."

"What else is wrong?"

"It turns out Chelle Curley is determined to rehab the derelict house in the Western Addition that the Kenyon brothers own."

"So let her strike a deal with them. She's a good negotiator."

"She's tried, but the Kenyons aren't taking her seriously — or at least Chad isn't. She's asked me as a special favor to intercede, and I don't want to deal with it."

Hy flopped down onto the sofa. "God, when the brothers took off for Europe I hoped we'd seen their backsides. And now we've got Flavio St. John after us."

"What!"

"He's filed a lawsuit, something about nonpayment for an 'exceptional and ageless' piece of art."

"He's full of shit! The contract specified that payment would be on acceptance of it by us."

"I've already turned it over to Hank. He said not to sweat it."

Hy's phone buzzed. He listened, made a

few curt replies, and hung up, then rubbed his eyes with the heels of his hands. "Oh, my God. You remember that trouble in Lima that I thought I'd wrapped up? It's come unraveled."

"Oh no! D'you have to go down there again?"

"Yes. ASAP." He explained what had happened.

My spirits plummeted. "It's not right. How can the CEO of a major corporation get himself kidnapped twice in the same place in the same year?"

"Good question. This time he's going to have to do some detailed explaining."

"When are you leaving?"

He checked his watch. "Depends on when I can get a flight. There's one that leaves in four hours."

"Okay, I'll carry on, e-mail anything important to you."

"Same here."

"One small favor," I added. "Will you please take the Kenyon brothers with you?"

12:31 p.m.

Chad Kenyon was very much with me, however. He had called Julia just as she was returning to her office from her morning's work, and in a moment of weakness she'd consented to setting up a luncheon for the three of us at Bella, his favorite Italian restaurant.

Why the hell had she done that? I'd asked.

Well, the Kenyons were good clients; they could put a great deal of money into the agency's pockets.

Why involve me? I'd asked.

She didn't want to eat alone with him.

Great. I was acting as a bodyguard for one of my own employees.

Now she sat beside me, wolfing her ravioli so she could get out of there as soon as possible. Ostensibly her reason was that the hunt for Renshaw was heating up and she needed to get back to it. In reality the hunt was stone-cold dead. Julia was in a hurry because she couldn't bear to watch Chad eat.

Chad loaded grated parmesan onto his linguini vongole. "Like I was saying, there's a fortune to be made in these derelict buildings if you know what you're doing."

I nibbled on a wilted lettuce leaf from the crab salad I already regretted ordering. Washed it down with a sip of pinot grigio.

"What's the matter?" Chad asked around a mouthful of pasta. "Something wrong with the salad? I'll make them take it back —"

"No, please don't. I'm just not very hungry."

"You should be like Sweetheart here." He gestured at Julia, who scowled at her plate. "She can eat and drink me under the table."

I smiled, nibbled on something green and curly that I always mistakenly call Caligula, then said, "I'd like to meet with both you and your brother to discuss Webster Street."

Chad's face darkened. "Don't get me started on that little weasel Dick. Soon's we got back from Europe, he's up to his old tricks again — sitting in the woods. Only now he's in so deep, there's no cell reception."

"He sits in the woods?"

Chad knocked back the rest of his wine and motioned to the waiter for another bottle. " 'Getting away from things' is how he puts it. Backpacks into some weird-ass wilderness and spends days — weeks, even — there. Says it brings him peace. What I call it is hiding."

I thought of Touchstone, Hy's and my place on the Mendocino coast, and the high desert sheep ranch he'd inherited from his stepfather. I could certainly understand the impulse.

"Hell," Chad said, "what's he want to hide from when there's so much action here?"

112

From you, maybe? I thought.

"What kind of action?" I asked.

"Where've you been living lately — in a cave? The city's exploding. Techies and all their lovely money are flowing in. Rents and home prices are soaring. Land too. You remember that hole in the ground on Russian Hill where you were investigating that witchy stuff last spring? I turned it over the day I got back from Italy, and there're already condos on it — a hundred percent occupied too. Families and poor people're heading toward the burbs, taking their damn dogs with 'em too. It's a goddamn renaissance!" He thrust out his arms, nearly swatting the waiter, who had returned with the wine. The server barely reacted; this was where Chad ate most of his meals, and the staff had become accustomed to him, I supposed.

"Dios mio," Julia exclaimed, "I'm going to be late for that meeting." She started to slide out of the booth.

"Come on, stay," Chad told her. "Have some of those raspberry tarts you love."

"No," I said. "She's officially on the clock for the agency now. See you later, Jules."

She fled before Chad could say anything more. I smiled inwardly, because I suspected she'd earlier asked the maître d' for a bag of the tarts — which she did love — to go.

So there I was, trapped with Chad, who was in the process of wiping clam sauce from his lips with his tie.

"I went to see that blighted building you hired me to investigate," I said, picking up the thread of our conversation from before Julia's departure. "I went by there yesterday afternoon."

"Yeah? What did you think of it?"

I'd decided not to tell him about someone pushing me down the stairs; he was likely to make a federal case of it. "It's really grim. I doubt you can sell it in its current condition."

He groaned. "Maybe I should've sold it to the Curley kid."

Reluctantly I told him, "She's still interested."

"Well, if I change my mind I'll get in touch with her. But she'd have to come up on the price."

"Other than that, there's been no interest?"

"Zip."

"Well, we'll try to secure it. Maybe then you can sell it for what you paid, even make a profit."

"Profit's what it's all about. But you know that."

It isn't, but the Chad Kenyons of the world would never believe that.

3:00 p.m.

Of all my operatives, only Patrick and Kendra were in the office when I returned from the horrible luncheon.

"Where're all the others?" I demanded.

"Out," Patrick said.

"I can see that. Where?"

"On the cases you assigned them."

"Oh." I consulted my calendar. "Okay, why don't we schedule a staff meeting for five o'clock then? Wind up the week."

"Shar, the weather's supposed to be really nice the next three or four days," Patrick said. "People'll be heading out of the city for the weekend. Or leaving work early and knocking back a couple of cold brews on their porches. I myself am leaving as soon as possible to take my boys to Lake County."

"Meaning not everybody's a workaholic like me?"

"I didn't say that."

"I told you when I hired you that sometimes we work twenty-four seven. What about the clients? Don't they need some satisfaction from us?"

He just looked at me. *Frustrated female,* his eyes said.

Well, maybe I was.

"Okay," I said, "we'll start out next week well. No meeting till nine o'clock Monday morning."

"Thanks." He disappeared into his office.

Kendra just sat there, her dark eyes conflicted.

"What?" I snapped.

"I could help out late —"

"No. You get an early start on the weekend too."

"But really, I could."

"Go!"

She nodded and fairly slunk out of the conference room.

Damn! Poor Paragon of the Paper Clips — I'd hurt her feelings by rejecting a gift she could scarcely afford to offer. Kendra has a large extended family at home, and her services as chief cook, cleaner, and caretaker are in high demand. Yet she always tries to pick up the slack here, staying late and issuing familial orders by phone: *The dryer is* not *busted; try cleaning the lint trap. Three hundred and fifty degrees is what you cook the casserole at. Don't give her the red pills! They could kill her. Hers are the blue ones.*

All of this delivered in a pleasant modulated tone — well, except when someone is

116

about to administer a potentially lethal overdose.

I went to my office, huddled in my chair
under Mr. T., and stared out at the Bay.

Had I turned into a temperamental boss?
A slave driver? Simon Legree?

No, I was just trying to hold my employees
to my own too-exacting standards. And that
wasn't fair. They had lives, plans, and
families — all of which I should respect.
And maybe I should learn to tend more to
my own.

But not until I took care of Renshaw, the
bastard. Not yet.

SATURDAY,
OCTOBER 10

5:45 a.m.

I was only dozing, but the cats were stone-cold asleep when Hy called. Neither animal so much as twitched when the phone rang.

"Where are you?" I asked groggily.

"Miami." He sounded exhausted.

"You've already wrapped things up in Lima?"

"I gave the bastard CEO hell, is what I did. Turns out he staged the threats against himself."

"Why, for God's sake?"

"Publicity for his firm, which he claims is going down the toilet. How he thought his being snatched again would improve their image or generate contracts, I can't fathom. Anyway, I severed our connection with him, and I'm about to catch an FBI charter flight to D.C."

"FBI?" Occasionally Hy consulted with them on hostage negotiations.

"Yeah. I had a voice mail from a deputy director while I was straightening out that mess in Lima. Very hush-hush hostage situation. I'll try to get home soon. And you know what? On the way here I came up with something that might explain why Renshaw's threatening us . . ." Short pause. "Look, McCone, the feds're signaling me. Gotta go. Call you from D.C."

"Good luck."

But he'd already broken the connection. I set down the phone and settled into my soft pillows. Whatever Hy had thought about Renshaw's motivation would keep a few hours.

Mist was drifting past the windows, and from the Golden Gate, I could hear the moan of the foghorns. A warning to ships at sea, they were a soporific to those of us on land. Within minutes I was asleep again.

9:15 a.m.

Hy hadn't called back from D.C., so I decided to go into the office. It might take my husband a long time to get back to me — as long as it would take for a delicate hostage negotiation to be concluded.

As I'd so ungraciously reminded Patrick the day before, M&R was a 24-7 operation, although on weekends only those immersed in important cases came into the office. Today Ted was there in the fourth-floor reception area, apparently waiting for me; he grabbed my arm and hustled me into my office as soon as I entered.

"He's back," he whispered.

"Who's back? Renshaw?"

"No. The weasel — Flavio St. John." He motioned at the surveillance monitor.

The artist was seated in the hospitality suite on the lower floor, dark eyes snapping with impatience as he stared fixedly at the door. *Weasel* was an appropriate description of him, I thought. His hair was black with orangey highlights; his face was narrow, with a pointed chin; his sharp little teeth protruded like a feral animal's.

Ted added, "He demands to know why you put a stop on his check. Apparently he's not satisfied with his lawyer filing suit against us."

"Tell him to go outside and look at the façade." I turned away from the screen.

"Shar, you've gotta do something. Otherwise he'll become a permanent fixture here."

"Call security."

"He told me that's what you'd say. He said he'd just come back and bring his attorney with him."

I was in no mood for Flavio's kind of

games. "This is the M&R building. If our security can't keep a weasel and his attorney out, we've got no right to be in business."

Ted smiled at me. "I'm not in the mood for his games either. Can I personally toss him out?"

I looked at his clothing: today he wore a familiar Edwardian theme. That velvet frock coat could not stand a scuffle. "In the interest of your wardrobe, call security."

10:54 a.m.

Flavio St. John was rousted by the security guards on our floor, and left, still yowling about a lawsuit. Peace descended.

Ted poked his head through the doorway. "You need some fresh air." When I didn't respond, he came in, took my hand, and pulled me to my feet. "Fresh air and some food."

"Where are we going?"

"To the roof garden. We'll order up from the deli."

I looked out the window, saw blue sky and sunshine; the fog had cleared without my noticing it.

Ted tugged at me. "Okay," I said, "but I want a big BLT — hold most of the green stuff."

12:31 p.m.

"So what's been happening while security's been busy repelling our intruder?" I asked Ted.

We were sitting on lounge chairs under a big blue marketplace-style umbrella. It was one of those days that was so clear you felt as if you could reach out and touch the Bay, the bridges, and the distant hills.

"Not a hell of a lot. The Paragon of the Paper Clips is busy this weekend. Patrick's away. Thelia's at her desk, but the others are out and about. Oh, and Lionel left a note that he's quitting."

"He's *quitting*? I just hired him two weeks ago!"

"Said he got a better offer."

"Well, why didn't he give me the chance to improve on it?"

"Face it, Shar, he's not worth any more than you were paying him."

I pictured Lionel. Mick was right: a shifty manner and furtive eyes did not make for a good investigator. Now that I considered him, I realized he reminded me of David Janssen as Dr. Richard Kimble in the old TV series *The Fugitive*. It was incredible that the fictional Kimble hadn't been apprehended the first time he wandered around looking furtive as hell.

125

"You know, I really didn't like Lionel much anyway," I said.

3:45 p.m.

Late in the day and I'd finished my paper-work, but I didn't want to go home. Lonely there, without Hy. Strange — we'd spent a great deal of our relationship apart, but somehow, after moving into the new house, I felt lost there by myself. An adjustment, I thought, to new surroundings. I'd come to terms with it.

But in the meantime, where to go?

The ocean. The place I loved best. And the home of two of the people I loved the most.

4:23 p.m.

I was walking along China Beach, feeling calmed by the rush of the waves. The fog was rolling in again, blurring the horizon and sweeping away the last faint colors of the setting sun as it tumbled playfully over and under the nearby Golden Gate Bridge. I breathed deeply of the cool, briny air, relished the mist touching my face. No mat-ter how many times I walked along the Bay or the sea, I would never lose my affinity for water. Once I'd listened to a pilot friend describe crossing Lake Michigan — really an inland sea — in her Cessna and resolved to do the same someday. A lot of pilots are afraid of flying over water; if you have to make an emergency landing, it's like hitting stone. But water has always been kind to me, and someday . . .

I'd come to the steps that led up from the cove to Rae's and Ricky's house on the bluff. Took them two at a time.

Rae Kelleher was my former assistant at All Souls and Ricky Savage was my former brother-in-law. Now Rae was a successful crime novelist, and Ricky's stock as a country-music star was still rising. Their Sea Cliff home on the bluff above China Beach had become a haven for me.

A haven that offered margaritas, which Rae was mixing in the blender. Mrs. Wellcome, their appropriately named housekeeper, who harbored aspirations of becoming an amateur sleuth, had been given the night off.

"They're not in season," Rae said of the margaritas, "but I feel like it's still summer."

"How come?"

"Got my latest manuscript off today. I'm now officially on vacation."

"Congratulations! Where's Ricky?"

"LA. Zenith Records is having a meltdown."

"A serious meltdown?"

"No, minor. But the boss must resolve the problem. Sometimes I feel like I married a traveling salesman — only he travels by private jet."

I looked closely at her. No, no signs of any problem. When Ricky had been married to my sister Charlene theirs had been a deeply troubled relationship; now they'd both grown up and found happiness with partners who better suited them. Still, I asked, "You ever think of moving down south?"

"God, no! Ricky can deal with the Hollywood nonsense, but he loves to escape it. As for me, this city is my inspiration — however ridiculous that sounds."

"I know what you mean."

"So, how's your work going?" Rae handed me a margarita, and I savored a sip before replying.

"Well, let's see. Gage Renshaw has surfaced."

"*What?* I thought he was dead."

"So did Hy and I. But he turned up in the office on Monday, looking more seedy than I remembered him."

"What does he want?"

"He won't say."

"What do you *think* he wants?"

"A piece of the business, maybe, although he denies it. To make trouble, in any case."

"He make any demands?"

"Not yet. You say you're not starting your next book for a couple of months?"

"Yeah. Why?"

"How about helping me out in the hunt for Renshaw?"

Rae often assisted me with my cases — her way, she said, of gathering material for her books, and keeping her hand in at her former profession. She'd always been great at tracking people down.

She considered. "Okay. I usually get pretty bored after I deliver a book. But isn't the PD doing anything about him?"

"I spoke with Larry Kaufman. He said he'd have somebody try to get a line on Renshaw, but I haven't heard back. Maybe they couldn't spare the man power."

"Wouldn't surprise me: short on money and perks, short on experienced personnel. I know Larry; I'll give him a call in the morning. We'll find the asshole, don't you worry."

9:55 p.m.
We'll find the asshole, don't you worry.

I thought about those words of Rae's as I drove home after a hearty dinner of her beef

129

stew. She'd told me years ago that she'd always be part of what my present staff insisted on calling Team McCone. And she'd proven it again and again.

Friendship. What creates it? What sustains it? Similarity of worldview, certainly. Good luck. Give and take. Mutual respect and trust. But there are many more indefinable components that make friendship a mysterious phenomenon. I've always been fortunate in my friends, as I have been in my family members and employees.

The cats were hungry when I got home. I wished that in this new neighborhood I could find someone as reliable as Chelle Curley to look after them when neither Hy nor I was home. But, I reminded myself, Chelle had grown up and now was well on her way to a career as a rehabber. I wondered if she'd persuaded Chad to sell her the house.

I still had reservations about the rehab job, but I'd had to learn to let my younger friends make their own decisions.

11:32 p.m.

For a while I tried to read. Several of my favorite authors had new books out, but my restless mind-set would have ruined good beginnings. I'd flicked through the TV menu, but nothing — current or old — piqued my interest. In between efforts, I'd tried to reach Hy at his various contact numbers, but with no success. Finally I shut off all the lights, wrapped myself in a soft afghan, and lay down on the living room sofa in front of the gutterings of the fire I'd earlier built.

Wind baffled around the chimney and occasionally sent little puffs of ash against the fire screen. The four yew trees planted across the house's façade scraped rhythmically. Close by, a dog woofed, and I frowned, recalling Chad Kenyon's remark about families with children leaving the city for the burbs and "taking their damn dogs with 'em too." The comment smacked of one of the many changes in San Francisco that concerned me. What was a city without families? Without its children, pets, playgrounds, and parks? What was a city where everyone flashed platinum cards but looked as if they'd just hopped off a Google bus?

We used to see elegant old ladies in hats and gloves, strolling in Union Square or lunching at elegant bistros off its alleyways. Elegant gentlemen too, rushing from one important appointment to another. Many of the well-known street performers — mimes, musicians, singers, orators — had faded away. Neighborhoods were becoming indistinguishable, and people who should have known better — given the fancy labels on their beer and wine bottles, pizza and sandwich containers — had taken to dumping their post-picnic trash without regard for amply provided refuse bins in our parks.

My thoughts about the city were making me sad, so I wrapped the afghan tighter, closed my eyes, and focused on the day ahead. First thing, try Hy again. Then, when he told me what he thought Renshaw's motivation was, I'd move on.

■ ■ ■ ■

Sunday,
October 11

■ ■ ■ ■

8:22 a.m.

I dialed Hy's cell as soon as I felt coherent in the morning. The call went to voice mail. Now, that wasn't like him at all. He always picked up for me. Unless he was involved in a dangerous situation . . .

Stop it, McCone! He's in D.C. at the request of the government.

Well, maybe there is *something to worry about after all. Our government . . .*

Why did I always feel like a miscreant whenever the government invaded my life? I paid my taxes on time; I voted faithfully, although I wasn't sure what good it did; I even contributed — minimally — to my candidates' campaigns. But there it was, that guilty, hunted feeling.

Time to get going. But why? It was the day of rest, as my adoptive mother called it.

Thinking of Ma reminded me of my entire family — now *that* is a confusion. My birth

135

mother, Saskia Blackhawk, is a nationally known attorney and advocate for Indian rights who lives in Boise, Idaho. My birth father, Elwood Farmer, is a prominent painter who lives in the Flathead Reservation in Montana. I have a half sister, Robin Blackhawk, in law school at UC Berkeley — my alma mater — and a half brother, Darcy Blackhawk, a deeply disturbed man whose whereabouts vary according to whatever institution his current doctors think will give him the best treatment.

Saskia was unmarried and unable to support me when I was born, so she allowed Ma and Pa, relatives on my maternal grandmother's side, to adopt me. In those days people weren't as open about adoptions as they are now, so I grew up thinking I was their natural child, my very different appearance a genetic "throwback" to my Shoshone grandmother. It was an act of kindness on Pa's part to leave me the documents that helped me discover my real heritage.

Something thumped downstairs on the front steps. The *Chronicle.* I could wallow in that for a while. I tossed on a warm robe and went down to grab it and start the coffeepot. But it wasn't the *Chron.*

It was Jill Starkey's rag, *The Other Shoe.*

136

I didn't subscribe to it. What was it doing here — and two days late at that?

With foreboding, I unrolled it and looked at the front page.

Main headline: "Seafood, Anyone?"

Local private eye Sharon McCone and her husband, Hy "Mr. Mysterious" Ripinsky, have egg on their faces — or is it clam chowder?

The recent renovation of the façade of the vintage M&R building on New Montgomery Street involves a sculpture by the famed and talented (???) Flavio St. John of Rome, Italy. A giant clamshell by St. John that is suspended over the building's classic entryway attests to the low-level taste currently prevalent in our city —

I screamed in rage and threw the offending newspaper across the room. The hideous little troll had struck again! I wanted to storm over to her shabby offices on Market Street and throw her butt out the window. No, I wanted to throttle her with my bare hands. How about torturing her first? Yeah, that was it! Matches, pins, needles . . . too bad I didn't know more about waterboarding —

"Starkey . . . shit . . . argh . . ." The cats were standing in the doorway to the kitchen, staring at me as if I'd gone insane. I silenced myself before I could make any more ridiculous noises.

The worst thing about this situation was that I couldn't get my hands on the troll because it was Sunday.

Sundays I'm always on call in case any of my operatives need me, and sometimes I drop into the office. I feel the need to check on everybody's progress; besides, my appearing on the scene tends to energize whatever operatives are working that shift. But mainly I prefer to dedicate the weekends to Hy — if he's in town — and when he's not to leisurely activities: trips to the Marin County Farmers Market; long drives in the country; brunch at a favorite restaurant and then a nap; matinees of movies I missed the first time around.

But all I could bring myself to do today was browse through the *Chron* — when it finally arrived — and rattle around the house, trying, as Elwood Farmer often said, "to assemble my thoughts." Every attempt collapsed like a structure made of pick-up sticks. I kept calling into the office to check on the Webster Street surveillance, to which I'd assigned a couple of freelance operatives we frequently used. Nothing was happening. I checked for messages from Hy, but there was nothing. Renshaw was leaving me alone — tormenting me again.

8:18 p.m.
I picked at Anne-Marie's pesto chicken, lost the thread of my conversation with Hank and her. We'd gotten together, as we often did on Sundays, for an informal dinner, but I couldn't focus. It didn't help that Habiba wasn't there, amusing us with chatter about a science project or speaking in French, which she was learning with great speed.

"How's Habiba doing at Mrs. Herber's?" I asked.

"Great," Hank said. "They built a kite this week and after school tomorrow they're taking it out to fly on Ocean Beach."

"Is that wise?"

"Flying a kite? You just run along, and a puff of wind —"

"You know what I mean."

"Shar, you can't keep a kid cooped up because of something that *might* happen. Besides, Mrs. Herber is a crack shot and will be armed."

139

My eyes filled with tears. I excused myself and headed for the bathroom.

It wasn't bad, as bathrooms go. Hanging plants and plush towels and interesting little soaps and hand creams. Of course it would be, since the flat where we were having dinner was Anne-Marie's.

She and Hank are one of those rare couples who can't live together — she's meticulous and he's an utter slob — but they've recognized the dysfunction and taken steps to rectify it. He lives upstairs in their two-flat building in Noe Valley, where he can inflict as much wreckage as possible; she lives downstairs in a place that looks straight out of *Architectural Digest.* Habiba travels happily between floors according to her mood, although I'm of the opinion that she secretly prefers Hank's squalor.

After a while I returned to the table. Nobody commented on my absence; they knew part of what was troubling me. Desserts had been placed before my plate: Napoleons. I wolfed down two and felt better.

At least I felt better until, an hour later in the car, I tried to call Hy's cell to bring him up to speed. Again I got no answer, not even voice mail.

I pulled to the curb; I couldn't think this

through while driving. Hy had been out of touch since the early hours of Saturday morning, when he was about to meet the FBI charter in Miami. It made me wonder if a hostage negotiation had gone wrong. Well, there was one way to find out: Craig. He kept lines open to his former colleagues.

I was about to phone him when the cell vibrated: Chelle Curley.

Chelle's voice was unsteady. "My boyfriend — Nemo? You just met him? I think he might be in trouble."

"What kind of trouble?"

"He's been acting so strangely — well, actually he's always been strange, you know the kind of guys I'm attracted to — but tonight, God, I don't know."

"Strange in what way?"

"Um, obsessive, maybe."

Great. "Obsessive about what?"

"That house on Webster Street. Ever since he joined the rehabbers and found out I was trying to buy it, he's been after me about it. Tonight your friend Chad called and told me he was thinking about accepting my offer. Nemo was all excited, told me it was as good as ours. Which it isn't — it's as good as *mine,* and only mine. We had a fight, and he took off, and I think he was going over there. With all those weirdos who hang out in it, I'm afraid for him."

"Did he say why he wanted to go there?"

"No. And he told me in no uncertain terms not to follow him."

"Why the urgency?"

"I don't know. He got a call on his cell, and then he just went manic."

"What's his cell number?"

"I don't know. It's a new one, and he never told me."

Oh, Chelle . . .

"Can you intercept him and keep him safe?" Chelle asked. "Please!"

"He didn't give you any indication of who the caller was or what the call was about?"

"No. He can be so secretive sometimes. He's hooked on spy novels."

"Chelle, how long have you known this guy?"

"Not very. Maybe about a month. He answered one of my ads for rehabbers. I kind of . . . betrayed my professional standards. No messing around with the help, you know?"

"Yes, I know. Does Nemo have a car?"

"An old Toyota Camry. Gray and beat-up, with a big dent on the passenger side. But last I knew it was in the shop."

"Okay, don't worry. I'll go over and see if he shows up. If Nemo should call, tell him

I'll be there."

Parking was plentiful near the derelict house, but as I cruised by looking for the Camry Chelle had described, I couldn't spot it. Maybe it was still in the shop and Nemo was coming on public transportation. I pulled to the curb and looked for any sign of the freelance operative who was supposed to be on the job tonight. There was none. Last time I used him, for sure.

No lights showed within the house, and there was no one visible on the property. The entire block was quiet too, except for the usual nighttime barks of dogs and honks of horns and screeches of tires on pavement. Tendrils of fog were sweeping in. Before long the mist would blur and distort my view of the house.

Maybe Chelle had misheard or misinterpreted what Nemo had told her. Or had she overreacted? She *did* have a lively imagination. Still, I'd promised her I'd wait for him. I'd have to loiter here until he showed or it became obvious that he wasn't going to.

The headlights of a passing car briefly illuminated the chain-link fence across the street, and I thought I saw something bulky move in the misty darkness near the hole in

143

the fence. Someone coming out. A kid who'd been in the house looking for creepy kicks? An adult squatter on his way to buy food or drugs? It could even be an animal, perhaps one of the raccoons whose dominance in the city was being challenged by coyotes, foxes, and even bears driven from their natural habitats by drought and incursions by humans.

I rolled down the window for a better look. Human, not animal. A blocky figure just emerging through the hole in the fence. The figure was tall and had a long stride, probably a man but I couldn't tell for sure —

There was a sudden flare of light in one of the house's front windows.

The dark figure didn't pause or look back, but instead broke into a run.

I flung myself out of the car, just in time to hear a whooshing noise come from inside the derelict building. The flare brightened behind both front windows, flickering wildly.

Fire!

The running figure was a third of the way down the block now. I didn't hesitate, but took off after it. My cell was in my coat pocket; I pulled it out as I ran, dialed 911. No immediate answer — the emergency response time was slow as usual. Behind me the foggy night was now stained a dirty red-orange and billows of smoke rolled skyward.

The fleeing man reached the corner ahead and turned west. I couldn't close the gap between us; running in high-heeled suede boots with a cell pressed against your ear is no way to win a footrace. Emergency answered, put me on hold. I switched off the phone as I neared the corner, shoved it back in my pocket. No need for me to tie up the line now.

Others would have called this in.

I turned the corner just in time to see the figure cross the street and veer into a narrow alley between a closed bakery and a dry cleaner. Who the hell was he? A squatter or neighborhood kid who'd set the house ablaze by accident? Nemo, who'd arrived before I did and been in the house all along?

Clattering, clanging noises sounded from the alley as I neared it — the fleeing person banging into and upsetting something like a garbage can. I pulled up at the alley's mouth to catch my breath. More sounds in the misty blackness ahead, not as loud. Then silence, except now I could hear the oncoming wail of sirens. All I could make out in the alley was vague shapes: garbage cans, piles of cast-off junk. No way could I catch up to the fleeing person now. I'd probably break my neck if I tried to rush blindly through the cluttered passage.

Damn!

The sirens' wails grew louder as I made my way back to Webster Street. By the time I neared the derelict house, firefighters were on the scene and more were arriving. The house was sheeted in flames, burning fast and hot the way old firetraps always do. There was no way I could leave; fire trucks and helmeted men unrolling hoses had my car blocked. All I could do was stand off at a distance among the usual rubberneckers that seem to come out of nowhere whenever a disaster happens. A few hecklers were there too, trying in their malicious stupidity to disrupt the firemen's efforts.

Why? I wondered, as an ambulance pulled up. Was it that they enjoyed being part of wanton destruction of property?

Don't contemplate the human condition now, McCone.

Those firemen who weren't manning the hoses were holding the spectators back and setting up barricades. A pair of police cars, sirens screaming and lights flashing, joined the melee, and the officers took over crowd control.

There wasn't much the firefighters could

do except prevent the blaze from spreading to neighboring houses. It wasn't long before the derelict building's roof caved in with a loud booming crash, sending up showers of sparks and embers. The rubberneckers made the kind of excited noises the Romans must have made during the gladiator matches in the Colosseum.

Suddenly I was drawn back to the night my own house on Church Street had burned down. I leaned back against something — a wall, a stoop? I couldn't tell through the numbness that set in.

Images flickered before my eyes: choking smoke, rising flames, frightened cats under the bed where I couldn't reach them. The first breath of fresh air as I yanked the outside door open. The searing pain when a post from the upstairs deck railing fell on my arm. Lying there in the damp grass and staring up at the smoke-filled sky as the flames claimed my home and almost everything I cared about. All because of a disgruntled client from years ago, whose case — except to him — hadn't been all that important or cost him any more than he deserved.

Now the acrid smoke and odors of burning wood and fire retardants made my eyes and throat hurt. The heat from the glowing remains seared my skin. The hissing of streams of pressurized water, the cries of firemen, cops, and onlookers rang in my ears. There was nothing I could do but keep on standing there, watching the old house die the same fiery death mine had.

■ ■ ■ ■

MONDAY,
OCTOBER 12

■ ■ ■ ■

2:15 a.m.

The first thing I did when I got home —
naturally — was feed the cats.

Before they would go to their bowl, they
sniffed suspiciously at me, and Alex retreated under a table while Jessie's tail
puffed up. People claim cats have short
memory spans, and maybe they do, but the
odors that clung to my clothing and hair
must have called forth visions of the fire in
which the three of us had nearly lost our
lives.

Next I got on the phone and called
Chelle's mobile unit. She answered groggily, sounding as if I'd awakened her.

"Where are you?" I asked.

"In my own bed at Mom and Dad's," she
replied in a sulky tone. "Nemo stood me
up, the asshole."

"Where were you supposed to meet him?"

"At a friend's place in the Sunset. She

gave me a key and told me to use the flat while she's visiting her folks in Indiana."

The lives of young people like Chelle and Nemo struck me, as they often had before, as nomadic. Few possessions, no permanent addresses, no connections except through electronic devices that might or might not work. Granted, I myself hadn't lived a conventional life, but I'd always felt grounded. Maybe younger people like Chelle and Nemo felt grounded in their freedom. But where had Chelle gone when Nemo hadn't shown up? She'd left the borrowed flat in the Sunset and gone home.

She seemed to come fully awake then. "Did you see Nemo?"

"Uh, no. He didn't show."

"Then he's a double-dog asshole."

"I wouldn't say so. Chelle, there was a fire. The house burned down."

She gasped. "My God, was anybody hurt?"

"I don't know."

"Nemo . . . he didn't have anything to do with it, did he?"

"I don't know that either."

"Then why hasn't he called me?" Her voice was spiraling upward in pitch.

"There're plenty of good reasons —"

"Shar, I've got to stop talking about this.

I'll call you back later." She broke our connection.

I went upstairs, stripped off my clothes, and stuffed them in the hamper. Then I took a shower, vigorously washing my hair. A good comb-out, body lotion, and a touch of the Allure perfume Hy had given me for my birthday last month, and I felt back to normal. That is, as normal as a woman can feel when she can't contact her husband, has just witnessed a horrific fire, and has a maniac breathing down her neck.

Thinking of Hy, I went to my laptop and dashed off an e-mail to Craig, asking him to contact his former colleagues at the FBI to see if any of them knew about Hy's presence in D.C. and why a deputy director had summoned him there. Then I crawled into bed. Five minutes later the landline rang. I picked up, hoping to hear Hy's voice.

Gage Renshaw.

"Out late, McCone."

So he'd been trying to reach me, but not leaving messages. Or he'd been watching the house and waiting for me to go to bed. "I had business to attend to."

"What kind of business?"

"None of yours." Quickly I depressed the control Hy and I have on our home phone for recording calls.

He said slyly, "Putting out fires, maybe?"

"I don't know what you mean, Renshaw."

"I'll give you a hint: Webster Street."

"What about it?"

"Are you tracing this call?"

"We don't have that capability on this line. Now what about Webster Street?"

"You were there."

"How do you know that?

"I know a great many things that you wouldn't expect me to."

"Are you following me? Or having me followed?"

He cackled in that annoying way he had. "Hell no. Why would I do something like that?"

"I wouldn't put anything past you, if you had something to gain."

"But I don't. Or do I?"

"Damn you! Why don't you tell me what it is you're after?"

"Because I like to keep you guessing."

"Guessing games are for children. I don't have time for them."

"My, you've turned into a sour bitch since I first knew you."

"Don't call me again until you're ready to talk sense. No more games!" I clicked off the phone.

As I was having my first cup of coffee, Mick called my cell. "You seen the news?"

"You know I don't watch TV news in the morning."

"Where are you?"

"Home."

"Well, turn on CNN and call me back."

"If this is about the fire last night, I was there —"

"Just check it out, okay? Sounds like it was arson."

When I turned on the TV, CNN was reporting on a suicide bombing somewhere in the Middle East. A collapsed building, an old woman crying, a child bleeding in his mother's arms. I looked away from all that misery until I heard the anchor's voice say, "In other news, the investigation continues into the fire that consumed a deserted house in the Fillmore district of San Francisco last night, killing one."

Killing one. . . .

I looked back, listened more intently. The anchor was one of those perfectly made-up, every-hair-sprayed-into-place women, and she was smiling. Actually smiling!

The picture switched to the house sheeted in flames.

"Fire chief Danielle Albin said the cause

of the blaze has not yet been identified, and arson has not been ruled out. A body found early this morning by fire inspectors sifting through the site was burned beyond recognition. . . ."

A body, burned beyond recognition. It wasn't only the house that had died in the Webster Street conflagration. Someone trapped inside it had died too.

Who? A squatter? One of the neighborhood thrill-seekers? Nemo? For Chelle's sake I hoped not.

8:10 a.m.
I picked up my cell and called Chaz Witlow, an old friend from college who was on the city's fire commission. As I'd expected, because of last night's fire, he was in his office.

"I was just about to call you," he said. "You were spotted by a couple of our personnel at the fire on Webster Street last night — how come you were there? On a job?"

"That's confidential."

"Come on, Shar, this is me you're talking to."

"All right. I have a client who owns that house and we were running a surveillance on it because it had been plagued by intrud-

156

ers. From what I heard on the news, it sounds as if you've already decided it was arson."

"There's evidence that points that way. The house was an open invitation to fire-bugs."

"I agree. When I toured it, there were piles of debris all over the place. One flick of a Bic, and fire would spread very rapidly. Did your investigators find any evidence of accelerants?"

"Not yet. But the fire appeared to have several points of origin. If it wasn't arson, I'd be very surprised."

"And what about the body that was found there?"

"No identification yet. It was a real crispy critter."

"That bad, huh?"

"That bad."

"Chaz, there must've been two people in that house when the fire started. I saw somebody running away from it just seconds before the flames flared up."

"You get a good look at them?"

"Not good enough to identify him."

"But you say 'him.' Are you sure it was a man?"

"Reasonably. He had a man's stride."

"Height? Weight?"

"Over six feet. He ran like a heavy man, but I couldn't tell because he was bundled up in a dark parka and jeans. He wore running shoes."

"Like half the men in this city. Any markings on the parka? Team or club names?"

"None that I saw."

"All right. We'll get onto it. I'll keep you posted, and if you remember anything else, call me."

9:22 a.m.

Kendra nodded at me when I entered the offices, and returned to whatever she was typing. I went down the hall to my private space and curled up in my chair under Mr. T., contemplating the brilliantly green Marin headlands. Until recently the hills had been browned off from last summer's heat and drought, their oaks and eucalypti and bay laurel standing out in sharp relief against long grasses that resembled wheat. Now patches of green showed through. It was another nice day. The morning commute was winding down, although cars moved slowly on the bridge. Waldo Grade was backed up in both directions as people left the city and vice versa. Used to be the heavy traffic was inward bound in the morning and outward bound at night, but in

158

recent years the volume had become about equal, as many businesses had spread to the suburbs.

As I sat there, I began to feel lower and lower by the minute. I missed Hy. There had been no news of him from Craig. I wished we were together at the ranch or the seaside. But then I've wished for any number of things; some hadn't happened, but a lot more had. Not bad, on the average.

10:07 a.m.

A knock on my office door. Mick stuck his head inside. "May we come in?" Then he walked in anyway, bringing a short, wispy-haired man in stained cargo pants and a rumpled T-shirt with him. The man looked nervous; he twisted the Giants baseball cap he held in his thick fingers.

Mick said, "This is Lester Harwood. He's . . . he used to be a serial arsonist, and has written a book about his experiences called *Firebug.*"

I blinked. "Uh . . . great. Please sit down."

Mick motioned the man toward one of the sofas. "Les decided to give up his profession before his luck ran out. His book is a tell-all under a blind pseudonym that will be published next spring."

Harwood remained standing, as if at at-

159

tention. "Should've gotten a bigger advance," he said in a rusty voice.

Where, I wondered, did Mick find these characters?

Harwood cleared his throat and went on. "You're probably wondering why I agreed to talk to you, Ms. McCone. It's not that I expect payment. But if the details of our conversation and a plug for my book should appear in the local media, I would be grateful."

Publicity hounds bark constantly in our society. I glanced at Mick; he nodded encouragingly.

"I can't guarantee it, Mr. Harwood, but I do have contacts with press people."

"So Mr. Savage here told me. You want information on arson, I'm your man." He sat down, seeming to gain confidence. "You know there are two kinds of arsonists?"

"Amateur and professional?"

"Right. In my lifetime I've been both. Now I've turned into a truly legitimate professional."

"And what does a truly legitimate professional arsonist do?"

"*Former* arsonist. I'm a consultant for three of the biggest insurance companies in the country."

Talk about turning a criminal activity into

an asset!

Lester continued, "Let me go back to when I was an amateur — eight years ago, as I recall. I always knew I was ready to start a fire when my fingers started to tingle."

"Tingle."

"Yeah. Sometimes I'd see something that reminded me of fire, and the old tingle would start. I've always been fascinated with it."

"With the tingle?"

"No, fire."

"What about fire fascinates you?"

"The way each blaze has a personality all its own. How it spreads in certain ways, and not always like you expect it to. It's as if it thinks. It's got *power.*"

"And does creating fire give you a feeling of power?"

He pondered that. "I *do* feel more powerful after I set a blaze — I mean, I used to. But now I got this good legit job and my book coming out. I guess I owe it all to fire, huh? I mean, before, I had no high school diploma, no family, no friends. No woman either. What kinda woman was gonna look at me? They all thought I was a nerd."

I did too — a dangerous one — but I said kindly, "I'm sure they didn't all think that way."

161

"Yeah, they did. A couple of them even told me so."

"And your reaction to rejection was to set fires."

"Why not? At least it was something I liked to do."

"What about the people you might have hurt?"

"I always made sure that the buildings were clear beforehand. Never made a single mistake."

"What about the occupants' possessions?"

He looked blank for a moment. "That's just stuff. You can always replace stuff."

I thought of the irreplaceable things I'd lost when my house on Church Street was torched: old photographs, scrapbooks, diaries, love letters, and much more. No, you can't always replace "stuff."

With an effort I kept my voice even as I said, "You have any things you'd really miss if you lost them, Lester?"

"Listen, lady — until I got this consultant's job I lived on the second floor of an abandoned warehouse. Never mind where. I'd heat up cans of baked beans and hash and soup on my so-called neighbor's little gas burner. I'd share my food with him because it was his propane I was using. The cans came from wherever I could five-finger

162

'em. My clothes I stole from Goodwill. You think *stuff* matters to me?"

Evidently not. His small eyes watched me. I wondered if Mick had told him about my history with arson, and he was deliberately goading me.

"Right," I said, "so you set fires for pleasure and power, not for money."

"*Used* to set fires."

"And how did you get this job with the insurance companies?"

"My upcoming book. And word gets around, who's a good torch. Insurance companies like the bad guys on their side. Believe me, I been approached by all sorts of policyholders to torch their property — some of 'em pretty high-toned."

"Such as?"

"Uh-uh. I protect my clients — former clients."

"Then your book isn't a tell-all?"

"No, ma'am. I don't name names or give locations."

I glanced at Mick; he was leaning, arms crossed, against a file cabinet.

"Ever set a fire on Church Street?" I asked.

Too quickly, Lester said, "No."

"How about Webster Street?"

"Wasn't me."

"Do you know who might have set it?"

"Not anybody I'd care to name. On the surface it seems like an amateur's work, but professionals sometimes arrange the scene so it looks like an amateur's work."

"Let's go back and pinpoint the differences between amateurs and professionals more thoroughly."

"Pros try to select a point of origin where the fire will have sufficient fuel and ventilation. Piles of flammable materials, open windows — they're good sources for a blaze that'll spread real quick."

I thought back to my walk-through of the house. Remembered the debris and the broken windows. Of course they didn't mean the blaze had been started deliberately — the person I'd seen running away from the house could have been someone who'd inadvertently set the fire by dropping a cigarette or match. Or someone who'd ignited it on the spur of the moment, for whatever reason. Wouldn't a pro have used a timing device that would ignite the blaze when he wasn't around?

When I voiced the question, Lester had an answer: "Sophisticated ignition devices are mostly seen in the movies. A flick of a Bic on fuel-soaked items is enough. Timers leave debris that makes it easier for investigators to pinpoint where the fire started, and may give away the identity of who put them together."

"How?"

"Every torch who works with timers has a method of building them — they call it a signature — that law enforcement catches on to and looks for."

"So how did Mr. Savage find you, Lester?"

"You better ask him. Guy's got smarts. You oughta keep him around."

"I intend to."

Lester stood and winked at me. "I like this neighborhood. Think I'll scout around, see if there're any places that're ripe for a hot burn."

11:41 a.m.

Mick said, "Shar, he didn't mean it!"

"How do you know?"

"He was joking."

"Was he?"

Mick shrugged, his expression conflicted.

I asked, "Was Lester the one who torched my house? Instead of the other firebug who went to prison for it?"

"No."

"Are you sure?"

"I asked him. The guy, in case you didn't notice, is a piss-poor liar."

165

"You're right about that. Where on earth did you find Lester?"

"He was hanging around outside of that old bar we used to go to on Valencia Street — Rusty's, remember? Looking forlorn because the place is dead, and watching all the affluent techies pass by on the way to the clubs. I felt sorry for him, so I went up to him and we talked about how the neighborhood has changed."

That was Mick for you. He'd been one of the first "affluent techies" in the city. He and a few others like him had fueled a revolution that had vastly changed San Francisco's culture.

"Anyway," he added, "Les and I went for beer at one of the neighborhood's last dives, and we've been tight ever since."

"Tight? You and that creep?"

"He's got possibilities as an informant. In spite of his new legit job, he still likes the old green." He made a motion with his thumb and fingers as if passing on a bill.

1:51 p.m.

I was enjoying a couple of slices of pizza — pepperoni, Italian sausage, and mushrooms — downstairs at Angie's Deli. Thank God Angie's a purist; pineapple, kale, goose liver, wine-soaked cherries and other such embel-

166

lishments have never been allowed to touch her thin beer-batter crust. A tiny woman who emigrated from Genoa decades ago, she's a fierce defender of her native cuisine.

Enter Patrick. I looked up at him in surprise and said, "What're you doing here? I didn't tell anybody at the office where I was going."

"I'm psychic." He sat down and ordered a glass of wine. "I had some free time this morning, so I did some research on the Webster Street house. You know I'm a member of the Old California Society?"

I nodded. The society is an association of history buffs.

"Well, I went to our members-only site and checked up on the place. There's a little-known rumor that things of value might have been hidden in there."

"Credible rumors?" I asked.

"Mostly."

"What kind of valuables could've been hidden in a place like that?"

"Nobody agrees on that point. Gold, silver, cash, valuable paintings — although I kind of doubt that paintings would last, because of the dampness."

I thought this over. It seemed far-fetched. Still, it was a possible explanation for all the recent interest in the place.

"Okay, fill me in on the rest of the story."

The rumors of hidden valuables, Patrick said, began in the mid-1980s. Two men, claiming to be representatives of a corporation called SIW, and their attorney had appeared in the city's civil court and petitioned for ownership of the Webster Street house. The proof they presented was skimpy and their request was turned down.

"You have court records?" I asked Patrick.

"On my computer. I'll shoot them over to you."

"Who was the judge?"

"John X. Williams."

Williams, who'd died a few years ago, had had a reputation as a strict interpreter of the law. My friend — well, former friend — Glenn Solomon had been a buddy of his. Perhaps Williams had discussed the case with him. Problem was, Glenn and I hadn't spoken in quite a while, ever since he'd lured me into a case and then deliberately neglected to provide me with important details.

Glenn . . . one of the foremost criminal lawyers in the country. Big, white-haired bear of a man. Married to a special woman, Bette Silver, an interior designer. They'd been my good friends, a go-to couple like Rae and Ricky, Anne-Marie and Hank, until

168

I'd found out he'd lied to me, compromised one of my investigations — and nearly cost me my life. And he hadn't thought he'd done anything wrong.

That was what still hurt the most: he hadn't thought he'd done anything wrong.

Bette had tried to bring us back together, but we are both stubborn people and her efforts didn't work. Finally she withdrew from the fray, not exactly siding with her husband — she was not one for favoritism — but lost to me anyway. I missed her friendship every day.

"I can't talk with Glenn," I said to Patrick.

"I know. I can."

"Will you?"

"No problem."

"Thank you, Patrick."

"You're welcome. Mick asked me to tell you there's a file on your e-mail. More background on the Webster Street place."

As it turned out, there was a *lot* more background.

In the late 1980s, William Acton's only living daughter, Chrysanthus Smithson, her husband Nathan, and their son Adam were planning to move from an apartment on Clay Street to the Webster Street house. Furnishings and major appliances had already been delivered, but the Smithson family didn't appear on the appointed date. A later investigation revealed they'd been last seen crossing the US-Mexican border in their old VW bus. The reason for their disappearance quickly became obvious when Smithson's San Rafael firm, Diverse Investments Management, reported the theft of three and a half million dollars' worth of bearer bonds that had been under Smithson's control.

A massive search had been mounted for the missing family and the bonds. There'd been no trace of them, or evidence that the bonds had been cashed in either the United States or Mexico. Swiss and offshore banks, in spite of their strict privacy requirements, had stretched their limits to assure authorities that the bonds had not been deposited with them. Someone had to know where those bonds were. . . .

4:50 p.m.

"Nothing so far on Hy's whereabouts," Craig said when I stopped into his office, "but I'll keep on it."

"Thanks. I'm not in panic mode yet, but . . ."

"I doubt it's anything serious. Things get muddled at the Bureau; one hand often doesn't know what the other's doing."

"But how can they lose the whereabouts of a whole *person*? And why hasn't Hy contacted me?"

"I admit the lack of contact isn't like him. It could be the kind of sensitive assignment that calls for strict silence. Or it could be a Bureau foul-up. I wouldn't be surprised if someday they lose the director himself."

I snorted. "Fine folks we're entrusting our interstate crimes to. Anyway, I've got something else to ask you: what do you know about bearer bonds?" Craig was my best advisor on governmental affairs, and while with the FBI had been assigned to numerous cases involving the Treasury Department.

"Hmmm." He paused thoughtfully. "Unregistered securities — meaning they belong to whoever possesses them. Very easily negotiated. But mostly a thing of the past: the government became aware that they were being used by tax evaders and money launderers, so in 1982 new issues were banned. As of last year, most of those bonds were extinct."

"But if I had some now . . . ?"

"If they were issued within the past fifty years with a long maturity date, you could redeem them at a cooperative bank or processing center. Otherwise you could use them to help you kindle a nice fire."

"Could they be redeemed in another country? Such as Mexico?"

"Depends on the bank. And the credentials of the bondholder."

"What if they were stolen from a large securities company?"

"Circulars must've gone out from the securities company and the government when the bonds were found missing. But then, as we know, people don't always read them until it's too late. Or they don't read them at all."

"Interesting. Thanks, Craig."

Those three and a half million dollars in bearer bonds had once been inside the house on Webster Street. I'd have staked my reputation on it.

6:10 p.m.

I'd read through the file Mick had e-mailed me several times, and waited around the office hoping Patrick had been able to speak with Glenn Solomon and would report back on their conversation. But it was nighttime and full dark: time for folks to tuck themselves into their homes, remote controls close to hand, or order out for pizza or Chinese, or stand in line for stage plays or first-run movies, or glam themselves up for an evening on the town.

None of which appealed to me.

I shut off my desk lamp and swiveled to look out at the Bay and Marin headlands. In the darkness lights winked on and shimmered, as if infused by sudden heat. The scene failed to entrance me as it normally did. I felt a stirring of the old restlessness that had initially lured me into my profession.

Where to go? Whom to badger with my endless questions?

I called Chad Kenyon's home and cellular numbers. Office number just in case he was a workaholic like me. No answers. What could he be doing? Eating. Where? At Bella.

8:01 p.m.

He was seated alone in what the maître d' had told me was his "exclusive" booth, a half-full bottle of Chianti and a single glass in front of him. His face drooped in unhappy folds, and he stared down at the table. When I slid into the booth, he didn't seem surprised to see me.

"You bring Sweetheart?" he asked.

"No, just me."

"Ah, what the hell, you're an old married lady. I can do better — anyplace, anywhere."

Yeah, sure.

173

"I know," I said. "And I'm not here to come on to you."

"Thank God. Then why, huh?"

He didn't seem very interested in an answer. Instead he motioned to the waiter. "A glass for the lady, please. And another bottle too." He fell silent for a moment, then looked up at me and sighed. "You're here about the fire, I suppose."

"Yes."

"I didn't have anything to do with it."

"I didn't think you had."

"Hell of a thing to happen."

The waiter placed a glass in front of me, and Chad filled it nearly to the brim. "Drink up," he added.

To please him I sipped. "Chad, a few days ago you told me that you didn't want to sell the Webster Street house. But then you called Chelle Curley and told her you might consider it. Why'd you change your mind?"

He shrugged. "The kid seems so eager and ambitious. She reminds me of myself when I was young."

"When you bought it, did you know about the stolen bearer bonds that might've been hidden there?"

He raised his eyebrows. "How'd you find out about them?"

"We've got an excellent research department."

"Well, yeah, I knew. Truth is, that's one of the reasons I bought the dump. It's an old urban legend. I didn't really believe it, but it kind of intrigued me. I've been waiting for this workman I trust to finish up a big job so I could bring him in to renovate it and look for the bonds. If the rumors were false, I'd just sell the place to the kid at a small profit."

"And now it's too late."

He didn't reply.

"Chad, where did you hear this legend?"

"Shit, I don't know. I get around. Sooner or later I hear most things."

A sudden inspiration came to me. "Since you hear so much around town, have you recently heard of someone who's out to get Hy and me? Someone who's been out of town for a long time, part of it in South America?"

He frowned. "You guys've got a lot of enemies. So do I. I mean, anybody who's successful is bound —"

"No, I mean somebody who's carrying on a big vendetta."

"South America?" He frowned again. "This wouldn't be one of your husband's former partners, would it?"

"Yes — Gage Renshaw."

"That sleazeball? I thought he was dead." Pause. "Well, maybe I've heard that he might not be quite as dead as some people claimed he was."

My patience with him shattered. "Christ, Chad, how can a person be 'not quite as dead'? You either are or you're not!"

"Okay, okay." He held up his hands as if to shield himself. "I've heard he's back in the Bay Area."

"From whom?"

"Like I said before, I get around. I don't remember all my sources."

"The hell you don't!"

"Okay. Guy's name is Tilbury. James Tilbury. A few years ago he was named the sexiest man in California."

What did that have to do with anything? "You have a number for him?"

"I did, but I forget it."

"Chad, I've heard from Julia that you have a memory like a steel trap."

His fleshy face fell into sorrowful lines. "It's the truth, McCone. I'm getting old. Stuff doesn't stick in my mind like it used to. Maybe I oughta just give up and go sit in the woods like my brother."

"Phone me with the number. Then you

can go sit in the woods." I slid out of the booth.

"Let's do this again real soon. Make sure to bring Little Sweetheart along."

■ ■ ■ ■

TUESDAY,
OCTOBER 13

■ ■ ■ ■

7:11 a.m.

Tuesday began much as any other day would. I slept until the cats ambushed me, purring and bumping my face with their noses. When I didn't respond immediately, Jessie got up on my chest and stared me in the eye. There's nothing worse than a stare-down with a hungry feline. Finally I said, "Okay, you'll get your breakfast." And then, just to frustrate them, I went to take a shower.

Half an hour later we were all enjoying our repasts in the breakfast nook of the beautifully tiled kitchen. Given my cooking abilities, I really didn't deserve such a marvelous space, but I was steadily improving. I'd mastered pea soup and was now studying up on Chinese cashew chicken. Next, an Irish stew! If anything, I was ethnically eclectic.

But this morning we were respectively

181

breakfasting on Friskies kibble and Special K. I don't much care for an early meal, but when I wake hungry, I go straight to the cereal boxes. The sun looked watery, the day promised to be cool; I'd have to dress snugly for my luncheon with the sexiest man in California.

Before I'd left Chad last night, he'd unearthed James Tilbury's number from his memory — displaying that strange pop-up recall most of us have — and called him to introduce me.

"Gage Renshaw?" Tilbury said. "Yes, I mentioned to Chad that I'd seen him on the street last week with Don Macy, a man who used to do odd jobs and sometimes drive for me."

"Do you remember which day it was?"

Tilbury hesitated. "I'm pretty sure it was last Monday, in the early afternoon, maybe about one o'clock."

"Where?"

"On Market, near New Montgomery."

Not far from our building. And Monday at one was when he'd appeared at our offices.

"Ms. McCone, I have to go out now. May we meet later and discuss this in person?"

"Yes. When and where?"

"One o'clock? On Union Street, El Diablo? I'll buy lunch."

"It's a date."

12:59 p.m.

James Tilbury *was* sexy. Not the sexiest man in California — I consider Hy the holder of that title — but tall and blond and well made, with a quirky smile and startling blue eyes. Heads turned as he stood up from his table at El Diablo and shook my hand.

He was having a Bloody Mary, and I agreed to the same. Once we were settled, he said, "I've heard of you, Ms. McCone. In fact, I've seen you on the news and in the papers."

"Too many people have. It's a drawback for an investigator. But I suppose being labeled 'sexiest man' is a drawback for you."

"Well, it's helped my modeling career, but I don't enjoy all the public attention, like here, for instance." He nodded toward people who were eyeing us from a nearby table.

"Who do you model for?"

"Anybody who asks. It's a living and a good one, but my agent still has to cobble various jobs together. Newspapers, catalogs, TV commercials. No film jobs — I haven't gotten that lucky, and I suspect I can't act

183

anyway. I once did a short film for the Jehovah's Witnesses, who were trying to attract the youth market, but they decided I was *too* sexy, and shelved it." Again the quirky grin. "You, now: is everything the press says about you true?"

". . . Yes and no. They always want to make a big deal out of things that aren't."

"How do you handle that?"

"Pull my head into my shell like a frightened turtle. Seldom give interviews. A few years ago I caved in to a documentary film company who followed me around for a week. It was the dullest week of my career. Absolutely nothing happened, and they scrapped the film. I was relieved."

"Understand perfectly."

"How about you? How did you get that sexy man title?"

"My agent entered me in a contest; there weren't a lot of other contestants, so I won."

"I think you're being overly modest."

He grinned at me and raised his hand for the waiter to bring us another round of Bloody Marys. Then we got down to the purpose of our meeting.

3:10 p.m.
By the time I left the restaurant, I was stuffed with mushroom enchiladas and had

considerable information on Don Macy, Tilbury's former driver and jack-of-all-trades, but very little more about Renshaw, whom Tilbury had met only briefly. Macy had lived over James Tilbury's garage on Russian Hill until late last year. He'd been congenial, efficient, and a good driver until he left his job without notice, taking along a pair of heirloom gold candlesticks from the house. The candlesticks were later recovered by the SFPD from a South of Market pawnshop, where Macy had let them go for a paltry one hundred dollars. Macy had by then vanished.

Tilbury had no idea where Macy lived or what he was doing now.

"And frankly, I don't care," he added. "I got the candlesticks back, and I don't enjoy spending time in court and writing checks to lawyers."

"Amen to that."

When Tilbury and I parted, he promised to be in touch if he remembered anything else about Don Macy or Renshaw.

As soon as I got home I checked the answering machine. No messages, even from Ma, who likes to call any- and every time the impulse strikes her. Nothing from Hy. This silence was driving me crazy but I, with Craig's help, had put out all the possible feelers. Unless . . .

I went to my laptop and brought up the address card page for my friend Sally Guthrie, who worked for the FAA in Oakland. After we'd exchanged pleasantries, I explained the situation. "Is there any way you can find out if Hy actually got on the charter the FBI had waiting for him from Miami to D.C.?"

"It'll be tricky — secrecy, secrecy, you know — but I can try. Let me get back to you."

"Thanks, Sal." I broke the connection, feeling empty and cold.

I started toward the kitchen, and the phone rang.

"Ms. McCone?" The female voice was vaguely familiar. "It's Emily Parsons, from Webster Street. I found an undeveloped canister of film that I think contains the photograph of the family who were going to move into that old house. My mom must've forgotten to get it developed."

"That's great. May I have it developed for you? I'd return the other photos, of course."

"You don't need to do that; Mom always takes too many pictures on vacation. But, yes, please stop by. I'll be here the rest of the day." She paused. "And anyway, there's something I need to talk with you about.

One of my boys saw the person who pushed you down the stairs there. He didn't speak up because he thought I'd punish him for being there before you fell."

4:01 p.m.
Todd Parsons said, "He was one of those sleazy guys we see around there at night." He was leaning against his mother, looking much younger than his ten years. She smiled encouragingly at him.

He went on, "All the kids in the neighborhood are afraid of him. He growls, spits, makes like he's clawing with his grubby long fingernails."

"Is he young? Old?"

"Old. Has a long white beard, not much hair or many teeth."

Probably one of the remaining former patients ejected from the state mental institutions when Reagan-era politics forced them to shut down. Nowhere to get food, shelter, or health care. And often dangerous — both to themselves and others. He must have pushed me because he was afraid of being caught in the house.

"Thank you, Todd," I said. "You've been very helpful."

"You're welcome," he said, looking at his mother for her okay for him to leave us.

Before he did, he turned to me and added, "And thank you for the chocolate you gave us."

I said to Emily, "You're raising a great pair of kids."

"We try. In this world all you can do is try."

5:25 p.m.

"Uh-huh," Patrick said. In the red glow of the safelight, he was watching an image emerge on a sheet of photographic paper in the developing solution.

We had a darkroom in our offices, but my skills at developing and printing were pretty rusty. Fortunately Patrick, our resident photographer, had still been there when I arrived with Emily Parsons's film.

The emerging image showed three people: a couple who looked to be in their late thirties or early forties and a boy, probably eight or nine. In the background I recognized the steps of the house on Webster Street. The woman's hair was long and blond and flipped back in a wedge style; she wore tight jeans and a T-shirt that accentuated her slimness. The man, also slender and similarly dressed, had dark-brown locks that curled around the nape of his neck. The boy: just a kid with a crew cut, wearing ripped jeans and a striped tee. The Smithson family?

"Patrick," I said, "when did photographs start having date stamps on them?"

"Uh, the eighties, I think."

"Are there any on this particular roll?"

"No, but there wouldn't be; the stamps are put on after the pictures're printed."

"Oh, of course. What's on the rest of this roll?"

"Scenic views."

"Of where?"

"Judging from the red rocks, I'd say Sedona. Some of the other backgrounds are mountainous — maybe Yosemite. Typical tourist shots."

Just as Emily Parsons had said.

"Can you print up a few dozen copies for me?"

"No problem. I'll just sharpen up the tone on this one and run it through the Xerox. In the meantime, how about catching some dinner?"

"Sure. Let's walk over to Miranda's."

Miranda's. It used to be the agency's waterfront diner of choice, but then the genial host had died and an incompetent daughter had taken it over, and later sold it to a less competent woman. The service and food had deteriorated. But tonight I didn't feel up to going farther away, and I really wasn't dressed for any of the better restaurants in the area.

Miranda's, however, was shuttered and had a big CONDEMNED sign over the door. The little waterfront building looked forlorn. I stared at it, thinking how the port was changing: shipping had long ago decamped to the better facilities at Oakland across the Bay; seamen's hotels had been revamped into luxury establishments; even Pier 24 1/2 — where our agency had had its offices for several happy years — was being demolished. Chic shops, expensive restaurants, and wine bars predominated. And now Miranda's, one of the last holdouts, was gone. Sinbad's, a similar establishment, had closed last spring. Would the venerable and famous Red's Java House be next?

We ended up going to one of the trendy and expensive restaurants that have sprung up near AT&T Park. In addition to being a wonderful place to take in a ball game, the stadium has breathed new life into what used to be a pretty seedy part of town and, in spite of my nostalgia, I enjoyed the changes. But lord, how I'd miss Miranda's!

8:09 p.m.
When I got home I found a message from

190

my friend Sally with the FAA. She'd found no record of an FBI charter flight out of Miami to D.C., she said. Added, "Not that it's surprising. They're such secretive bastards."

I was huddled under a quilt on my sofa in front of the fireplace, trying to work out a scenario about the disappearance of the Smithson family and the bearer bonds, when the doorbell rang. I opened it to Michelle Curley. She looked distraught, her face tear-streaked, her hair wild in the wind that swept down the narrow street tonight.

"He . . . he's dead. He was the one killed in the fire."

"He? Who?"

"Nemo."

I pictured the blond, bearded man Chelle had introduced me to last week. "How do you know that?"

"The coroner's office identified him from his dog tags."

"He was in the military?"

"Yeah. I'm not sure which branch — he didn't like to talk about it."

"Why did the coroner's office call you?"

She ran her fingers through her hair. "I've been bugging them about an identification ever since you told me about the fire. Bugging the city parking control too. I finally

191

found out Nemo's car was towed from a green zone two blocks from that horrible house last night. I knew the body was his. I just knew it!"

I motioned her into the house, where she sat on the sofa without taking off her coat. It was misty outside and fine droplets clung to its waterproof surface. I eased her out of it and hung it on the hall tree where it could dry.

I said, "Do you want something to drink? Soda, juice —"

"What I'd like is a straight Scotch. Double."

The request surprised me; somehow I often forgot that Chelle was an adult now. I'd have to drop the parental attitude. I went to the kitchen and fetched the Scotch, bringing along a glass of Chardonnay for myself. After I'd stirred up the fire, I sat next to her.

"It'll be warmer in here soon."

She didn't respond.

I added, "Let's talk about Nemo for a while."

She nodded, staring into the flames. At least I wasn't losing her attention completely.

"Nemo James," I said. "It's an unusual first name. Years ago, people named their kids Mary and John, William and Susan; then it was Kevin and Tracy, Jason and Kendall. Now a lot of new babies' names're made up, or designed to recognize important people or events in the parents' lives. My favorite's Gunnip, the son of a client who was introduced to his wife by a friend with that surname. The kids in school have already taken to calling him Gunnysack."

"Shar, you don't have to natter on to amuse me. I'm not about to fall apart. I just need somebody to talk to."

"Okay, I'm sorry. What do you know about Nemo?"

"I told you the other day, not much."

"Date of birth?"

"No."

"Place he was born? Or where he grew up?"

"He told you he was from Utah. That was the first time I'd heard that. I always assumed Southern California."

"Why?"

"He just sounded that way. You know — American as apple pie, but with a touch of Spanish accent. You talk that way yourself."

I guessed I did, and I'd been up north for decades. Proves you can't lose all your background characteristics.

"What about education?"

"He said he went to UC San Diego for a couple of terms. Majored in earth sciences, but he left because he couldn't afford it."

"And after that?"

"He came up here."

"When?"

She shrugged.

God, what was *wrong* with her? With the dangers of date rape, STDs, and plain craziness, people today were usually careful about whom they hooked up with. But Chelle, whom I considered bright and practical in the extreme, had let this stranger into her life and bed — well, sleeping bag — without knowing the bare facts about him.

I asked, "How did you meet Nemo?"

"He answered one of my ads for rehabbers. I'd put it on my Web site that I'd be needing extra help if I bought the Webster Street house. I guess I shouldn't have publicized it, but I was so damn hopeful. And then, like I told you, I broke my own rule and slept with him. Stupid, really stupid."

"We all make mistakes."

She looked down and ran a hand over her brow, sweaty now from the flames. "Shar, do you think we could cut this short? I'm feeling pretty bad right now."

"Sure we can. You want to stay here to-night?"

Her tense face flooded with relief. "Can I? I'd really appreciate it. I don't want to spend the night in any of my buildings or the flat my friends loaned me, but I don't want to go home and tell Mom and Dad how badly I fucked up."

"You didn't fuck up, you liked the guy, and I could tell he liked you."

"But I didn't know anything about him."

"What, are you supposed to pay us to run a deep background check on everybody you spend time with? There were things I didn't know about Ripinsky till we were practically married. Probably still are."

Chelle looked unconvinced by my argument. "But my folks, they're so conventional . . ."

I tried not to smile, thinking of a few of the elder Curleys' youthful exploits that they'd confessed to me. "I'll call them and say you're helping me out around here for a few days. But right now you need your rest. Guest bedroom's upstairs, the second door on your left, towels and linens in its closet."

"Shar, you're the greatest!" She got up and leaned over to hug me, nearly falling on me in the process. Not inebriated, only tired. I watched her totter on the stairs, my heart going out to her.

So Nemo had received a call on his cell and rushed to the Webster Street house, cautioning her not to follow him.

Why? Did it have something to do with the bearer bonds?

One thing figured: the fire had been deliberately set. And that made Nemo's death murder.

Late as it was, I called Mick and asked him to run deep background on Nemo. He's always been a night owl, so he said he'd get to it right away. Then I went to bed and fretted until I decided to watch the late-night movie, hosted by a crazy man with furry black eyebrows and a fondness for rubber chickens, which the technicians on the set frequently hurled at him.

11:17 p.m.

The phone beside my bed rang. Hy? Or Renshaw again? I muted the old Bette Davis movie I was dozing to, and picked up.

It was neither. Rae, sounding excited. "Shar, I've been staked out at your building all day, and I've finally hit pay dirt. Early this evening I spotted Renshaw slinking around there."

Now I was fully awake. I sat up, turned on the bedside lamp. "What was he doing?"

"Trying to find a way in, I think."

"He still there?"

"No, he's been on the move ever since. It's a curious thing: each of the places I followed him to has been a building housing long-term document storage businesses. Classic Containers, Stor-for-You, Safety Systems, the Depot, Kelley's Warehouse, Secure Spaces. I lost him after the last one."

"And he acted like he was trying to get into them?"

"Yeah. He actually was let into Kelley's — it's a twenty-four-seven operation. Stayed quite a while."

"What the hell d'you suppose he's after?"

"Well, according to my research in the phone book, the places I named all store old files and documents for businesses. Listen to these slogans: 'Your secrets are safe with us.' 'Tighter security than Fort Knox.' 'The NSA has nothing on us.' I wouldn't trust any of them with the contents of our trash bin."

A memory was stirring in the back of my mind. When we'd merged our companies, Hy and I had decided to retain all our old paper files. Since there were so many of them, secure off-site storage was necessary. But I couldn't remember which facility we'd picked.

I asked Rae, "Did Renshaw have anything with him when he left Kelley's?"

"Nope."

"Okay. Thanks. You did good."

"I think I ought to get a gold star on my forehead. When he lost me I even scrounged the nearby Dumpsters to see if he'd thrown something in one. No results except rancid applesauce in my hair."

"I'll pick up some gold stars. Maybe some red and green ones for the holidays."

11:49 p.m.

Neal Osborn, Ted's husband, sounded wide awake when he picked up my call. "His Highness is sleeping," he told me. "I, of course, am sitting up late, putting Brodart dust jacket protectors on my latest purchases." Neal is a rare-books dealer with a worldwide mail-order clientele.

"Do you mind waking him?"

"You're the one who called. You wake him. I'll place the phone on his pillow."

Moments of silence; then Neal said, "Go ahead."

I did, and received a squawk from Ted that blasted my eardrum. "What the hell are you doing, calling at this hour?"

"After all these years you ought to be used to it." Ted and I had been together forever;

in fact, the first sight to greet me the day I'd been hired by All Souls had been his big bare feet resting on top of the reception desk.

He said, "Let me gather my wits — such as they are." Long pause, lots of moaning and snuffling. "Okay — what?"

"Quick question: what company did we contract with to store our out-of-date paper files?"

"You woke me up to ask *that*?"

"I wouldn't have if it wasn't important."

"Let me think." Another pause. "Duggan's? No, that's a funeral home. *D* something. Aha! The Depot."

"Can I get in to look at the files?"

"Sure. But there're a ton of them."

"I know approximately what time frame I'm looking for. Do I need to show ID or anything?"

"Your investigator's license and business card should do the trick. Most of them probably know who you are anyway."

"Thanks, Ted. Go back to sleep now."

"I've been asleep the whole time I've been talking to you."

■ ■ ■ ■

Wednesday,
October 14

■ ■ ■ ■

7:01 a.m.

I tried Hy's cell first thing in the morning and received no answer. I wondered if Craig's contacts from his FBI days had reported anything about his whereabouts or the reason for his ongoing silence, but I knew that if they had, Craig would have immediately been in touch with me. Unless the news was so bad that . . .

No, Craig would have informed me no matter what. If the worst had happened, both he and Adah would have been here by now, to try to cushion the blow. And if his former colleagues had had even a hint of where Hy was now, they'd have let me know, to give me hope. This was simply one of those wait-it-out situations, during which the one who did the waiting felt cold and helpless as a creature trapped in ice.

I shook the feeling off, pulled myself together, and drove to the Depot on Mission Street near the Goodwill Industries' outlet, arriving one minute after the storage facility opened. Already there was a long line of people waiting to get at whatever they kept there. After inching forward for several minutes, I was able to present my license and my request to the man on the door. Soon I was seated in a cubicle that resembled those in the safe-deposit vault at my bank, and soon after that a young guy with a hand truck hauled in and off-loaded four oversize file boxes, the top one covered in dust. He told me to press the buzzer under the shelf when I was done.

I blew the dust off the box on top and started in. By the time I reached the third carton, I was no longer sneezing, because the dust had settled, I thought — and then I realized the box had been wiped off and recently handled.

Maybe Renshaw had gained access to the Depot after all.

I pressed the buzzer and the same young man who had rolled the boxes in came to the cubicle. "Has anyone else asked for these files recently?" I asked.

"Not that I know. You want me to check our log?"

"Please do."

He went away, and I contemplated the file

box. What could be so important about our old records — ?

The man came back. "Nobody's asked for these since you stored them here, Ms. Mc-Cone."

"Are you open twenty-four hours?"

"No. Eight to six, Monday through Friday."

"What if somebody needed to get at their documents outside of those hours?"

"There's an eight-hundred number to call, and a guard will let you in. But it's only available to renters and there's a code they have to present. You must know that —"

"Normally my office manager handles document storage. You mentioned a guard. Does that mean there's only one on duty?"

"At night, yeah. I mean, who's gonna break into a place that's full of old papers?"

I could think of one. "What's the name of the guard who was on duty last night?"

"George Bender."

"You have a phone number and address for him?"

He hesitated. "You don't want to go bothering old George, Ms. McCone."

"Why not?"

"Well, because he lives up to his name. Bender. He's sleeping off one in a back room right now."

No, I didn't want to bother him; he probably wouldn't have made any sense.

"What about your alarm system?"

"Oh, that. It's pretty old."

"Is it hooked into the police or fire departments?"

"I don't think so. Like I said, it's kind of old. I'm not sure it even works any more."

The place was like a sieve. I said, "Thanks . . . I don't think I caught your name."

"Mac. You're not gonna report me —"

"No worries." Although I was going to get Ted started on finding a new document storage company.

Mac exited, and I turned my attention to the third file box.

10:24 a.m.

Finally I found a report written in blue ink in a crabbed hand that I recognized as Dan Kessell's. To my knowledge Kessell had never used a computer, probably owing more to secrecy issues than to his technological abilities. I suspected a great deal of what Kessell had undertaken in the guise of his partnership in RKI had been illegal.

Client: Diverse Investments Management.

Job description: Locate Smithson family,

206

formerly tenants of Webster Street home belonging to the family trust of William Acton, et al. See attached.

Family last seen crossing border at San Diego into Tijuana. Date, license plate #, make and model of van attached.

Objective: Do not notify authorities. Seize approximately $3.5 million in bearer bonds stolen from Diverse Investments Management, SF, and return to client.

There was no recommendation as to what should be done about the family.

I looked up and stared at the cubicle's blank white wall. While I was surprised my two cases were connected — one of those crazy coincidences that sometimes happen in detective work — I thought that I should have caught on to the fact before this. Should have at least suspected connections among Renshaw, the Webster Street house, the bearer bonds, and the Smithsons. Yet how could I have, really? The only association I'd had until now was the fact that Renshaw had taunted me about the fire, and that was tenuous at best.

Somehow Renshaw had found out about Kessell's long-ago case and come looking for details. Now he had discovered them, and was only a short jump ahead of me. How had he found out? Not from Kessell; the man had survived torture during the Vietnam War. The aura of corruption and danger that had since surrounded him had put even his worst enemies at a distance.

I thought back to Kessell's death: he'd been shot at close range with a .38-caliber handgun, survived without recovering consciousness, and died of cardiac arrest after extensive surgery. And then it had turned out that his entire existence had been a sham.

Could Renshaw have gotten close enough to Kessell to fire the fatal shot after forcing information about the bearer bonds from him? No, in spite of years of suspecting he'd killed his partner, I didn't think so now. For one thing, Kessell had known exactly what kind of animal Gage was. For another, if Kessell had given up the information about the bonds to him, why had Renshaw waited years before searching for them?

In any event, Renshaw's current activities were much more important. He'd known I'd been at the scene of the Webster Street fire. Now that I could link him to the bearer bonds, I suspected he might've been there too. Was it he who had set the fire, thus causing Nemo's death? Was he the man I'd seen running away and chased?

I flipped the file pages to the rear and found a page left blank for notes, onto which Kessell had scribbled the name Bernardo Ordway. And an address: 10 Via Enero, Santa Iva.

A few more pages were covered with Kessell's crabbed writing.

Again, Santa Iva.

I Googled the name on my iPhone. The only place I found with that name was a mere dot on the map halfway down Baja California Sur on the Pacific. Population: 1,570. Principal occupations: fishing and livestock.

Below Kessell's notation was travel information: Southwest to San Diego, flight 399, 11:55 a.m. Connection: Aeromexico to Santo Ignacio, flight 2, 4:37 p.m. Rental car: Hertz, confirmation number 54.

I checked Airnav.com. Santo Ignacio was the nearest airport to Santa Iva, but if that was his final destination, Kessell would still have had to drive about a hundred miles to the coast.

I wondered if Kessell had made the trip. Too late to find out, though: airlines and rental-car companies don't store such information very long.

Okay, if Kessell had made the trip, what, if anything, had he found out? And what the hell had happened to the Smithson family?

1:23 p.m.

I'd just called an emergency staff meeting for two thirty, the earliest Ted and I could get all my operatives together, when Patrick came into my office. His face looked pinched, as if he'd smelled something particularly nasty.

He said, "This morning I talked with Glenn Solomon. He claimed he knew nothing about John X. Williams or his judgment in the dispute of the ownership of the Webster Street property."

"That's bullshit! He was buddies with old John X. They talked almost daily."

"Maybe they only talked about their golf games."

"Glenn hates golf. He's not really into anything but the law."

"Yeah, well, now he's denying knowing anything about the case."

"I don't understand what's happening with him," I said. "He used to be like an uncle to me, but he's become an adversary."

"Would be interesting to know why."

"Heartbreaking is more like it."

"Want me to find out? I can."

"Not a priority." I wasn't sure I wanted to know Glenn's reasons for turning on me. "Why don't you help Rae out on trying to locate Renshaw? He's given her the slip again."

"Rae? She's working for us again?"

"Yeah, she's between books and claims she needs material for the next one."

Patrick shook his head. "Man, if I had her bucks, I'd be sitting around peeling grapes and spooning up the caviar."

"No you wouldn't."

"A moot point. Right now I'm scrimping to add to the boys' college funds."

I made a mental note to look up Patrick's employment file and see if it was time for a raise in his salary. He certainly deserved one, and as a single father of two adolescent boys whose mother was long out of the picture, he needed one. He managed to juggle the responsibilities of parenthood and his job with a skill that I found nothing short of amazing. Almost every week he had a tale of his new adventures with the kids, but I'd often caught him at the office late at night doing paperwork or on the phone. As a person who frequently forgets to tend to her cats, I was impressed.

As we entered the conference room,

people were assembling around the big round table — taking out files, pads, pencils, and laptops.

Once we were all settled, I said, "This vendetta Gage Renshaw has against us is heating up, and I've found a strong connection between it and another case — the Webster Street fire."

A few of them blinked and sat up straighter, and others made notes as I explained what I'd realized. They all looked as surprised as I'd been earlier, then contemplative.

"Our best lead to Renshaw is the only friend of his we've been able to identify — one Don Macy. They were seen on Market near New Montgomery by a reliable source on Monday of last week — the day Renshaw paid his visit to these offices. We have to make locating him a top priority. Unfortunately, we know very little about him."

"How little?" Adah asked.

Derek said, "We don't know where he lives or what kind of job he currently holds. He has no listed phone number or accounts with the water department or PG&E. No accounts with any cable TV or Internet providers either. No bank accounts, driver's license, or auto registration. No state identification, voter's registration, or passport.

Our search was Bay Area–wide, and we'll be expanding it to Northern California. Southern, if necessary."

"The invisible man," Patrick said. "Except he's been seen by a reliable source on the street with Renshaw — and not too far from here. Maybe Don Macy is an assumed name?"

"Could be," I said. "James Tilbury, the man who told me he'd seen him on the street with Renshaw, had employed him under the Macy name up until a year or so ago, but he told me in a phone conversation earlier today that he'd had an SSN for the guy and had tried to file a 1099 tax form with the IRS, but it was rejected for having too many digits."

"Can't this Tilbury count?" Derek said.

"How often do you count the numbers of your own, much less somebody else's SSN?"

"You got a point there."

We all were silent for a moment. Then I added, "As I said, finding out anything we can about Macy and locating him are our top priorities. I can't stress that enough. He may be our only key to Renshaw's where-abouts. Mick and Rae — between the two of you, you probably have the most infor-mants. Work them, and work them hard."

"I already have been," she said, "and I'm

beginning to pick up hints that some people have spotted him."

"What people?"

"Ones with street cred. For instance, Boo LaDoo — not his real name, of course. Boo's already stretching out his grimy tentacles. And Astro Turf. He lives in a Dumpster behind the Old Mint and knows every wino and druggie South of Market."

For a moment the outlandish names distracted me. "I once had an informant, Junk Yard Cat, who lived in a chain-link enclosure with seven garbage cans. He alternated nights in each of them. Mick, are you still having drinks with Lester, the reformed firebug?"

"Most every night. I'm his big bud now."

"Keep it up; I still don't think he told us all he knew about the fire." I swept the assembled faces with my eyes. "Renshaw is extremely dangerous. Physically he's gone to seed, but his mind is as sharp as ever. Please use extreme caution and discretion if you spot him. Call for backup from one of us or the PD if necessary. Now, our next issue is Nemo James, the man who died in the fire — any input?"

Mick spoke up. "I talked with the coroner's office. Their preliminary finding is that James died of blunt-force trauma to the head before the fire started. That's based on the condition of what was left of his cranium and the lack of smoke residue in his lungs."

"Murder, then."

"The PD's treating it as such."

"You get any additional information about James's past?"

"Some of it checks out with what he told you and Chelle Curley, some of it doesn't. There's no record of him being born in Utah. No record of any schooling before he did a couple of terms at UCSD on a now-defunct program for disadvantaged individuals. I asked for his records, but they've been disposed of. After that he enlisted in the army and was stationed at Fort Bragg, North Carolina. Was a clerk in their department of procurement, which sounds racy, but isn't — mainly means buying supplies like toothpaste and soap. Honorably discharged five years ago. After that he's not easy to trace. I'll keep trying."

"Do that, please," I said.

He nodded. "Now, about the stuff you found out from the RKI files, here comes the interesting stuff. I called that town in Baja — Santa Iva. Lousy phone service, but I managed to get hold of Pedro Santos, the chief of police, who speaks excellent English. He claimed not to know the Smith-sons."

"They might've been using an assumed name. After all, they were fleeing the US because they'd committed a crime."

"Normally I'd say yes, but the chief seemed nervous. Evasive too. He was lying, or at best distorting the truth."

"Why would he do that?"

"No clue."

"Mmm." I leaned back in my chair, con-templating the heavy blotter/calendar Ted had insisted on setting before each of our places at the conference table so we wouldn't gouge its rosewood surface with our frequent scribblings.

Mick asked, "How's your Spanish, Shar?"

"Not too bad."

"Maybe Chief Santos would be more open with someone fluent in his own language."

"What about *your* Spanish?"

"I've been away from it too long. It's been years since I lived near the border. I do bet-ter in cyberspeak."

"That doesn't surprise me."

"You've kept up with the language better than I have, though."

"It's been an effort, but I've always be-lieved that Californians need to be reason-ably fluent in both English and Spanish to

216

get along. The Hispanic population has topped that of whites in this state, you know."

"So it would follow that the people in Santa Iva would deal better with you. Especially if you spoke to them face-to-face."

Now I understood what he was getting at.

He added, "You look more like them too. I mean, the Indian blood and all. And you're really good at asking the right questions."

"But I can't just leave —"

"Yes, you can. You may have noticed that you've built up an impressive staff here. Team McCone can probably deal with your absence for a few days, weeks, months — maybe forever."

"Thanks, you little bastard."

Mick scowled. "You know, that's the problem between you and me. You started calling me obscene things when I was a baby, and then you went and dropped me on my head when I was only a few months old."

"As I've repeatedly told you, that was an accident. Besides, it's why everybody calls you a genius. Head injuries often produce interesting results."

"I might've been more of a genius if you

hadn't dropped me —"

"Shit happens, kid. Get over it."

The newer staff members were looking alarmed at this exchange, but the others were grinning.

Mick came around the table and hugged me. "You're all right, you know?" he said. "More than all right."

"Hey, don't destroy the McCone family legend. I'm the evil aunt, who intended to do you egregious harm. And you're the evil nephew, just waiting to give back as good as you got. Now everybody get to work."

Rae said, "Even me? I'm not even officially on staff."

"You're on staff. You've never left."

She grinned. "Nobody ever really leaves Team McCone."

Mick asked, "In the meantime, what'll you be doing?"

"If all goes well, when you hear from me next I'll be down May-hi-co way."

■ ■ ■ ■

THURSDAY,
OCTOBER 15

■ ■ ■ ■

4:33 a.m.

I had had mixed feelings about making the trip to Santa Iva. For one thing the landline, cellular, and Internet services probably weren't very good in remote Baja Sur. That would put me at an even greater distance from Hy should he try to contact me. The same with my staff, upon whom I so greatly rely for information. And the machinations of actually getting away for God knew how long were tedious. Fortunately, since Chelle was staying at my house, I didn't have to worry about the cats' being tended to. But I still had to check the weather in Baja and pack accordingly, and then there was the problem of how to get there.

Ted had tried valiantly, but he wouldn't have been able to book me on a commercial flight earlier than the next morning. So I'd called Oakland Airport's North Field, where we tied down our 170B, and asked if anybody was heading out for San Diego or Mexico and might be willing to take on a passenger who could spell her/him at the controls. Yeah, an old friend of Hy's, Bob Benson, who kept his plane at North Field, was making a late-night run into San Diego, and agreed to let me ride along. I didn't ask what he was carrying in the hold of his old Beechcraft Baron. I was better off not knowing, and he wouldn't have told me anyway.

In San Diego I found that there were no flights to Santo Ignacio — the nearest airport to Santa Iva — until late the next day, so again I asked around the FBOs and found another of Hy's ubiquitous friends, Trip Adams, who offered to take me to a small — very small — sandy beach strip a mile or so from town. He had a drop to make there and, after all, he said, he owed Hy a favor. Again I didn't ask what the drop contained; I was just grateful to be able to enter the country in such a way that I could conceal my .38 Special in my carry-on bag.

Still, as I often did, I wondered how many favors were owed my husband — and what had occasioned them.

6:13 a.m.
Trip Adams followed the Mexican coastal road — like ours, named Highway 1 —

along the ocean until it turned east into a thickly forested national preserve, and finally landed at the beach strip, which wasn't so much sandy as rocky. The rocks didn't faze him, however, and soon we'd made a relatively smooth touchdown and taxied to a stop next to an old red Honda Civic that was waiting there. The pilot introduced me to its driver, Enrique Valdez, who had done some work for RKI in the past, and — after accepting a few small packages from the driver — he loaded my small bag into its trunk and wished me a nice stay in Santa Iva. Valdez started for town, regaling me on the way with tales of his adventures with my husband.

"Oh, sure, me and those RKI guys go long back. Your husband is a real fine fellow. I remember the time in Guadalupe when we . . ."

I leaned back, shut my eyes and ears. Over the years I'd heard dozens of "I remember the time when" stories about Hy. Most of them were probably exaggerations or outright fabrications, but they were all flattering. If people wanted to tell them, that was okay with me.

8:11 a.m.
In Santa Iva we went to the small green

223

stucco building that housed the police station. The chief, Pedro Santos, with whom I'd spoken briefly on the phone last night, welcomed me into his office, where the walls were papered with US and Mexican wanted posters, most of them yellowed and out of date.

Santos was a young, slender man with what I call a lounge-lizard mustache. He smoked small cigars, lighting one from another. He seemed to harbor the feelings toward women that were prevalent in his part of the world, and examined my credentials for a long time, then quizzed me exhaustively about my qualifications. I sensed it was his way of putting off my questions about the Smithson family.

Finally I said in Spanish, "Señor Santos, I've probably been a private investigator since you were a child. As I told you last night, my husband and I own a prominent San Francisco agency, McCone & Ripinsky. Why are you concerned with my credentials?"

He flushed slightly, fidgeted, then continued the conversation in English. "I do not understand why you are here."

"Then why don't you ask me?"

A flicker of a smile played at the edges of his mouth. "Why *are* you here?"

"The Smithson family. And Señor Bernardo Ordway."

I'd mentioned the Smithsons earlier, but the name Ordway disconcerted him.

I went on, "Who is this Señor Ordway?"

"How do you know of Señor Ordway?"

"His name has been in my agency's files for many years."

"In connection with what?"

"What do you think?"

He looked away, didn't speak.

"Chief Santos . . ."

"Señor Ordway is an *Americano,* but has lived here for two decades. He contributes generously to the schools, the hospital, the libraries. He is *muy importante.*"

"What does Señor Ordway do for a living?"

Santos spread his hands widely. "He has independent means."

Probably a crook who escaped the States with his spoils.

Santos added, "As I say, he has lived here many years. He knows many people and many things. He is also a very private man; it would be very difficult to arrange an audience with him."

God, he made it sound as if Ordway were the pope! "Do many people seek audiences with him?"

"Very many."

"And are they all refused?"

". . . Not all."

"Tell me this, if you will: do you know a man named Gage Renshaw?" I described him in detail.

Santos considered, as if paging through a mental photo album. "No, I do not."

"Is it possible Mr. Ordway knows him?"

"Mr. Ordway knows many people from all over the world. I have no way of ascertaining their identities."

"Will you please speak with Mr. Ordway? Ask him to meet with me? Mention Gage Renshaw's name?"

"I will, *señora*. But I know what his answer will be."

I doubted Santos would even bother.

4:02 p.m.

By late afternoon I felt as if I'd brought the plague to Santa Iva. The mayor was unavailable to me. The Hotel de Ignacio had no rooms. The beer I was brought in a café was overly warm and full of foam. I decided not to return there for dinner; God knew what they would've served me.

Enrique Valdez seemed to sympathize with me, but that was probably due to my being Hy's wife. My command of Spanish intimidated him: gringas were not supposed to be so fluent. When I asked him if he could find me a place to stay the night, he pondered some, then drove me to an attractive stone-and-mortar house in a quiet part of town, the equivalent of a B and B in the States.

The room that Yolanda Ibarra, the pleasant landlady, showed me to was comfortable and airy. The bathroom was sparkling clean. I asked Enrique to come back for me at eight and then took a long soak in the claw-footed tub. Señora Ibarra had told me she would be playing cards at a friend's house till at least eleven, so I had the place to myself. I reveled in the quiet: a dog yapped outside, and a few ratchety motors drove past, but by and large, I could have been home in my big bedroom at the back of our house on Avila Street.

The thought of home washed over me. The cats, lonely in the absence of both Hy and me, either wrapped up together on our bed or wrestling in the way they do, which starts out as play and then turns into full combat. And Hy — a skitter of anxiety ran up my spine. Was he right now trying to reach me? He must know by now that I'd been trying to locate him. Usually, even when apart, we feel a strong psychic connection that tells each the other is all right, but it had faded as the days went by.

8:12 p.m.

I'd had a light dinner of tortilla soup at a café that Señora Ibarra had earlier suggested, and by eight was back at her house to meet Enrique Valdez. The driver had been eager to comply with my wishes all day, but when I asked him to drive me to the Ordway house, he scowled and thrust out his chin stubbornly.

"Strangers are not welcome there, *se-ñora.*"

"I can test the rule, can't I?"

"Test? What is this test?"

"To go up and ring his doorbell."

"You would only meet one of his *subordinados.* I have heard they are not very pleasant to strangers."

"In my business, Enrique, many people are unpleasant to me."

He let out a sigh that said he didn't want to be the one who facilitated the unpleasantness.

I relented. "At least take me to someplace from which I can observe his home."

"As you wish." Reluctantly he put the Civic in gear.

"Pardon me," he said after we'd left the town and were traveling across a flat land

228

where the distorted shapes of giant cacti dotted the desert floor, "but what do you know of Señor Ordway?"

"He seems to be *Señor Grande* around here." Mr. Big, Mr. Upstairs, as such characters are known in the old B movies.

"*Si, señora,* he is."

"And what do *you* know of him?"

He shrugged. "How is one such as myself to know someone of his importance?"

"Come on, Enrique. This is a small town; people talk."

"Me, I do not listen to gossip. It is for womenfolk."

I gave up and leaned back with half-closed eyelids, watching the terrain change as we drove into the eastern hills. Scrub grass gave way to larger fields of cacti, and then to profusions of flowering shrubs. A light scent floated on the air — jasmine? Another plant? I sneezed. Also pollen. I sneezed again.

The terrain became steep, and at the top of the mountainous slope a large two-storied hacienda-style house with a tiled roof and roughly plastered cream-colored walls loomed, awash in many lights. Music and laughter and voices filtered down. Mr. Big was giving a party. A half-circular paved area in front of the house was clogged with cars.

Enrique looked at me and made a helpless gesture. *"No hay entrada,"* he said. "There will be chauffeurs, parking attendants, perhaps security guards."

"None of them will be stationed this far down the hillside," I said. "Let's keep going until we find a wide spot where you can turn the car around. That way we can leave quickly if noticed."

He looked dubious, but complied.

The wide spot we finally came to was flat and paved. More importantly, it had an unobstructed view of a brightly lit terrace where music played and people mingled. A couple of newish cars were parked there. Enrique pulled between them.

"This," he said, "is where the help parks." In a bitter tone he added, "Look how far uphill he makes them walk."

Figures stirred in the cars to either side of us; two sturdy men in khaki uniforms equipped with shoulder holsters and rifles slung over their shoulders stepped out.

I stiffened and reached in my bag for my .38.

"No te preocupes," Enrique said. No worries. "These men are my *amigos.*" He added, *"Nada que temer."* Nothing to be

afraid of. He reached under the passenger's seat and removed a paper bag, handed it to the closest one.

"Jose Cuervo," he confided to me. "The tequila will be added to your bill." To the men he said, *"Media hora, por favor."* He added to me, "That will give us enough time."

I scanned the two-story white mansion. It had expansive windows angled to let in the brilliant colors of the setting sun. But massive bars on all of them would only serve to mar the view.

"Señor Ordway must be very afraid of something," I said, more to myself than to Enrique.

"He has reason to be. He has many secrets."

The party sounds grew louder as I got out of the car: laughter and muted conversation; faint music with a Latin beat; what sounded like ice blocks being smashed for cubes. A man's voice yowled; I guessed he thought he was singing. A woman's voice answered, screechy and off any key on the musical scale.

"I have binoculars," Enrique said. "Very powerful, left over from the days when I worked with those guys like your husband." He rummaged under the passenger seat and placed them in my hands. I wondered what other treasures that seat harbored.

I aimed the binoculars at the terrace with a low rock wall, sharpening the focus. They were of excellent quality, their definition strong and clear. Various formally dressed men and women, cocktails in hand, were visible beyond the wall. Waiters in white uniforms moved among them, offering canapés and trays of drinks. The yowling man had started up again. A tall gray-haired man put his hand on his shoulder, spoke into his ear. The yowler slunk off.

Enrique laughed slyly.

I said to him, "Can you pick Bernardo Ordway out of this crowd?"

He took the binoculars from me. "*Sí*. He is the tall one with the red carnation who just made the singer shut up." He handed the glasses back to me and guided them to follow Ordway's progress across his terrace.

Bernardo Ordway cut an impressive figure among his guests. As he moved, men shook his hand or clapped him on the back. Women brushed close to him, planted kisses on his cheeks, their formal gowns often flowing in the wind to envelop his legs.

I'd known many Bernardo Ordways: some had sought my investigative services, then attempted to take control of whatever case they'd brought me. Glenn Solomon, to my sadness, was one of those. Hy's world was riddled with them, all with some ulterior motive and a need for power.

More cars were arriving at the Ordway mansion. The guards, so far as I knew, were performing their jobs competently in spite of the tequila, but the parking area was filling up. When I mentioned that to Enrique, he said, "There are *otras* up the way to the house."

After a while, when I'd seen all I needed to, I tugged at Enrique's sleeve and we drove back to town.

■ ■ ■ ■

FRIDAY,
OCTOBER 16

■ ■ ■ ■

9:10 a.m.

In the morning I did the sensible thing in this age of advance appointments: I called Bernardo Ordway's office and asked for one.

"Why do you wish to see Señor Ordway?" The woman's voice was brusque.

"I'm thinking about buying a home near Bahia Tortuga" — a pricey community that spans the dividing line between Baja California Norte and Sur — "and given Señor Ordway's prominence in the community, I'd hoped he might advise me."

"Has someone referred you to him?"

"Yes, Pedro Santos." Surely the chief of police's name would have some influence, at least with Ordway's staff, if not with the man himself.

"Your name, please?"

"Judy Bolton." It was that of a heroine in a series of girls' mysteries I'd enjoyed during childhood. "You may have heard of me, or at least my family. We have large holdings in Central and South America."

Pause. "I will have to look at Señor Ordway's calendar and then speak with him. If you call back in half an hour, perhaps forty-five minutes, I may have an answer."

She'd probably check on the Bolton family, who, so far as I knew, lived on only in books and had no holdings anywhere.

The delay gave me time for a light breakfast — coffee and toast at my posada — and also an opportunity for a stroll around the plaza, which corrected my negative first impression of Santa Iva.

It was a typical small Mexican town: bodegas and fresh vegetable stands and small dwellings surrounding a central square; church spire dominating the skyline; children playing, mothers running after them; dogs pretending to be fierce. Old women in black dresses and shawls; young women in bright colors and jeans; old men smoking and gossiping on benches; young men smoking and ogling the girls. I caught no hint of the drug gangs that have made so much of Mexico a dangerous place for American visitors. Most of the faces I encountered were friendly, some openly welcoming. I exchanged greetings a number of times. Maybe I hadn't brought the plague to Santa Iva after all.

So why did the place still make me feel uneasy?

9:33 a.m.
I still had some free time before I'd been asked to call Ordway's office again, so I checked out the church: it was of a simple style, with whitewashed walls and wrought-iron chandeliers with electric candlewick bulbs suspended on chains. The unpadded wooden pews, as I remembered from my Catholic childhood, were hard enough to keep parishioners awake during the most uninspired of sermons. There were no elaborate stained glass windows, paintings, or statues; this was designed to be a place where opulence would not interfere between God and his faithful.

Out of deference to the few old women praying there, I covered my head with a silk scarf I found scrunched up in the depths of my bag and sat quietly, trying to clear my mind. The peaceful feeling that stole over me, I knew, was only momentary, but I valued this calm before the probable storm.

After I left the church, I noticed that Friday seemed to be a farm-to-market day: vendors were setting up stands stocked with fresh fruit, vegetables, preserves, and various crafts. People were beginning to arrive, many with drawstring bags, to do their shopping. I took another walk around the plaza, browsing at the stalls and buying a small framed woven cloth that I thought might make a good Christmas present for my sister Patsy. I also bought a wickedly grinning miniature of *el Diablo* for Mick, and a handsome woodcut of desert cacti for Alison. For Hy and me, I didn't have the heart to buy anything.

When forty-five minutes had passed, I phoned Ordway's office.

Got a busy signal. During my walk I'd noticed Via Chiflada — loose translation Crazy Street — where Ordway's office building was located, so I decided to go over there. The building took up most of a block and was three stories high, about average for this part of town, its stucco painted a disagreeable mint-green. Inside was a stark, empty lobby floored in faux marble squares. A flight of uncarpeted stairs led upward. I'd decided to act upon my principle of just showing up and taking the person by surprise, but the sounds of an altercation filtered downward.

Two voices, a man's and a woman's. My Spanish was good, but not enough to make out all the words.

". . . should not have told her to call back . . . no, not . . ."

"How could I . . . who she . . . no, I didn't . . . she . . . name was Judy . . . something."

". . . your brains, you . . . fool! I warned you . . . gringa asking questions in town . . . very dangerous."

The gringa obviously was me. This was not a good time to make a phone call to Mr. Ordway, much less pay him a visit. He'd been told about me, perhaps been given a description. If I was going to see him, I'd have to find another way.

I went back outside, took a table at a small café a few doors down the street, and ordered a Jarritos lime soda. The day had turned warm, but a breeze wafted from the plaza and stirred the hair at the nape of my neck. The breeze was refreshing and so was the soda, but they did nothing for my powers of logic. I began to question why I'd come down here, what I'd hoped to find.

For all I knew, I'd gone off on a tangent. The Smithson family might never have come here, might have nothing to do with my case. On the other hand, there were those three and a half million dollars' worth of missing bearer bonds, and Nemo, who had died in an arson fire.

A man was coming down the street: he

241

was dressed in a garish serape — gray with alternating stripes of red, yellow, and green — a tattered straw hat with a faded red band pulled low on his forehead, and incongruously shiny black loafers. Before he got to where I sat he turned into Ordway's building.

I felt a prickle of familiarity, so I stayed put while signaling to the waiter and settling my bill.

Fifteen minutes passed. Twenty. Then the man came back outside in the company of an older, distinguished-looking gentleman whom I recognized as Bernardo Ordway. The two walked to the plaza, talking and gesturing as if they were arguing. I followed at a distance. Soon they turned into a cantina.

I walked slowly past it, caught a glimpse of the interior through the open door: darkly lit with blue and red neon; a bar, several tables, a platform for a band, and a small dance floor. Quiet now in the somnolent afternoon. The men sat with their backs to me at a central table, beers and shot glasses of tequila in front of them. They were still talking, but less intensely. I couldn't see the face of the man in the serape clearly because the straw hat still obscured it. Ordway was clad in a pale-blue guayabera shirt. A few other men hunched at the bar, but I didn't see any women, not even those who might be prostitutes. Too early for them, I supposed.

That is a big drawback for women investigating in places like Mexico: you can't follow men into places like cantinas without being instantly noticed and observed more than casually. I would've given anything to get close enough to hear what Ordway and the other man were saying, but I was forced to loiter across the street, waiting for one or the other to come out.

11:19 a.m.
Finally they did, and I followed Ordway's companion back to the town square. At first the straw hat and serape made him easy to spot.

The plaza had filled with people. Adults milled about, filling their shopping bags; children ran unchecked or begged their parents for ice cream and candy. A band was setting up on a small platform, testing its audio equipment; screeches and voices cut through the air. From every side merchants hawked their wares: *Maiz tortillas? Nopales enlatadas? Frijoles secos?*

A little girl in a fancy pink dress ran in front of me; I had to grab her to keep her from falling. When I looked up, I couldn't spot the man I'd been following. I climbed up to the third step of the church, scanned the crowd. Not a sign of him.

Five streets branched off the plaza like spokes in a wheel. The man must have gone down one of them. Fighting through the crowd, I peered into the first to my right. It was more of an alley, really, containing nothing but overflowing garbage cans. In the second a young couple were caught up in an amorous embrace against a building's wall. I withdrew, started down the third.

A few yards away a pair of children — two boys, probably around eight or nine — were fighting over something.

"¡El mio!"

"¡No, mio!"

The object causing the dispute was the man's garish serape. The straw hat lay at the kids' feet.

I went to them and asked, *"¿De dónde has sacado esto?"*

They stopped tugging at it. One boy let go and put his hands behind his back.

"Is okay," I added. *"Puedes tenerlo."* You can have it.

The boy holding the serape turned and pointed at a trash can. *"Esta."*

"Who put it there?"

They looked at me blankly.

I translated my question into awkward Spanish.

"Esta," the boy said again, pointing toward the far end of the street.

Looked and spotted a tall man with a distinctive white shock of hair and shambling gait turning a corner.

Gage Renshaw.

"Gracias," I said, and ran after him.

There was no one in the side street, but I was certain the person had been Renshaw. And I felt certain Renshaw was here for the same reason as I: he'd read Kessell's notes in the file and was following up on them. His eccentric dress was obviously intended as a disguise, but from whom? No one in Santa Iva could possibly care that Renshaw was walking around the town — no one but me.

Damn!

I made my way back through the crowd to the church steps, sat down, and called Chief Santos's office. He himself answered.

"The man I mentioned to you earlier — Gage Renshaw — is here in Santa Iva. Is it possible for you to find out where he's staying?"

Santos didn't sound particularly interested, but he replied, "I can ask one of my officers to look into it, yes. If he learns anything, is there a number where I can reach you?"

I gave it to him, and we ended the call.

11:50 a.m.

After some consideration, I consulted my notes on the old Kessell file and asked a passerby for directions to 10 Via Enero. There were no names that I recognized on the mailboxes, but an archway opened into a small courtyard where a woman sat in a chair, alone. She was heavy, with what we used to call — before we were in danger of developing them ourselves — "batwing arms" protruding from her loose, garishly flowered red muumuu. Grayish blond hair was gathered on top of her head and secured with what looked like a pair of chopsticks. Even so, it straggled down on her forehead and the nape of her neck, clinging to her sweaty skin.

I edged closer. And accidentally stepped on a sprinkler head that clicked as it went down.

"Who's there?"

Busted. I stepped out onto the patio. "Sorry, ma'am. I took a wrong turn."

"Well, take a right turn and get out of here."

She didn't look at me. Her arms were blistered and peeling. Not the result of a bad sunburn, though; this looked like a serious skin condition. In spite of her south-of-the-border accent, she was an American. An American who apparently had lived here many years . . .

I took a chance and said, "Chrysanthus . . . you *are* Chrysanthus Smithson?"

". . . Yeah, I am. And who the hell're you?"

I handed her one of my cards.

She studied it, then set it down on the arm of the chair. "You're here about the bonds, I suppose."

That surprised me. If I had participated in a major theft, even many years ago, I wouldn't have been so forthcoming. But then, the statute of limitations had run out on the crime, so she probably felt she had nothing to fear.

She motioned to a bench across from her. "You may as well sit down."

I perched gingerly on its edge; it was old, with many protruding splinters.

"Who hired you?" she asked.

"I'm sorry — that's confidential."

She snorted. "Confidential!"

"Your old house on Webster Street in San Francisco —"

"What about it?"

"It burned down last week."

"Doesn't surprise me. It was a fuckin' firetrap to begin with."

"Don't you want to know if the bearer bonds your husband stole burned with it?"

"Those bonds — they ruined all our lives."

I took out my mini cassette recorder. "Do you mind if I make a tape of this conversation? I won't use it for anything but to help me recall the details."

She glowered at the machine. "You haven't told me who hired you."

"As I said before, that's confidential."

"Confidential, my ass!"

I decided to relent somewhat. "All right — a good man who's moved around a lot and bought the house because he wanted to settle down there." I pictured Chad Kenyon's sad face the last time I'd seen him. "He's heartbroken over losing it."

My choice of words was exactly right for Chrys Smithson; I'd sensed that beneath her hardened exterior she was sentimental. "Okay," she said, "turn the thing on."

I activated the machine. "Now," I said, "tell me about the theft and how it happened."

"Well, none of that's any secret. Nate took the bonds. He handled huge amounts of money, but it was all other people's. We never could put any by for ourselves. He gambled — you know how that goes."

"Yes. So Nate took the bonds . . . ?"

"In the early morning. And all of a sudden, it was get in our VW bus and take off. I didn't know a thing. We were living in an apartment on Clay Street in the city, but we'd decided to move into the Webster Street place as soon as our lease ran out. Our new stuff had been delivered and was waiting there. We'd unpacked a lot of it, even had one of our new neighbors take a picture of us on the front steps. But then Nate said we were going to dump everything and move to Mexico. After we were down here, Nate told me he'd stolen the bonds and hidden them in the old house. Later, when things quieted down, he'd go back for them."

"Why did he hide them?"

"He was afraid to cross the border so soon after the theft."

"When did he figure it would be safe?"

She shrugged.

"Did he tell you where in the house he'd hidden them?"

"No. He thought it was better if I didn't know."

"And he never even gave you a hint?"

"Not one. Nate took his secrets to the grave."

"Well, maybe it's lucky for you that he did: the authorities circulated the bonds' serial numbers immediately. Even if he'd tried to redeem them before the expiration date, he'd have been apprehended, and you might have been charged as an accessory."

"What's this thing about an expiration date?"

"Most bonds have a date after which the bearer can't cash them. Did Nate tell you when that was?"

"No."

"Did your son know about the bonds?"

"Well, sure. That's all Nate could talk about before he died. If we could only get at those bonds and cash them, all our problems would be solved. Right."

"Your son — where is he now?"

Long pause. "I don't know. My son is dead to me."

"Why?"

"No single reason. It's just that there's too much water under the bridge . . . over the bridge . . . whatever. But he was a sweet boy. And he had such an imagination. He was entranced with stories about pirates, and he'd pretend he was a character out of a Jules Verne novel, running around in a cape made of bedsheets with a broomstick sword covered in foil, yelling 'Ahoy!' After that it was cowboys and Indians, with him playing both roles. I always thought he'd grow up to be an actor or a writer, but now . . ." She shrugged. "What's going to happen to me? Are you going to report me and have me extradited and put in prison?"

"Of course not. You didn't actively participate in the theft, and the statute of limitations has run out by now anyway."

"That's something, I guess. Not much, but something. All anybody like me can expect in this life."

12:14 p.m.

I replayed the tape I'd made of our conversation for Chrys Smithson, then asked, "Have you ever heard of a man named Gage Renshaw?"

She frowned, then shook her head. "No. It's an unusual name, I'm sure I'd remember it."

"But you do know of Bernardo Ordway?"

"Why do you want to know about him?"

"He's connected with the man who owns the Webster Street house." A small fabrication.

"Well, he's a powerful man in these parts. And ruthless, rules the town. Maybe not

251

just the town. God knows how far his reach extends. People have been known to disappear in strange ways when they cross him. What he does is broker information. Man's like a sponge — sucks up stuff that he finds out and sells it to the highest bidder. He has informants all over the world, and I hear he spends a lot of time surfing the Net, trying to come up with dirt on people."

"Interesting hobby."

"Hobby? It's his profession. They say he makes millions at it."

"I see. Anything else about Ordway?"

"No. I told you all I know. I've never met the man. But you can be sure he knows all about *me.* He just doesn't bother me because there's nothing I have that he wants."

12:55 p.m.

As I was walking back toward my posada, feeling out of sorts and at loose ends, an old blue Toyota with rusted and chipped paint pulled up next to me. Chief Santos leaned out and motioned for me to get in.

"Am I under arrest?" I asked to test his sense of humor.

He flashed me a faint smile. "Should you be?"

"Somewhere, probably."

"One of my men went to Hotel Ignacio to

252

see if this Gage Renshaw is registered. There is nothing on record, and his description meant nothing to the desk clerks. There are a number of posadas near the square. My man called them. Señor Renshaw is not at any of them. It is possible he could be renting a room in a private *casa,* but we have no way of knowing where."

Probably he'd been staying at Ordway's villa. But for how much longer? For all I knew he was already on his way back to the Bay Area.

Santos lit one of his small cigars. The car smelled of them, a scent that warred with a pleasant gardenia perfume. His wife or lady friend obviously had good taste; I hoped she would prevail in the battle of the aromas — as well as save him from lung cancer.

"I checked with your San Francisco police about you," he said as we pulled away from the curb.

"And you found . . . ?"

"That you are a good investigator but *dificultoso.* Troublesome."

I couldn't argue with that; I'd given the PD plenty of trouble over the years.

"I would like to know all the reasons you have come to Santa Iva. Perhaps then I can help you. Shall we go to a place I know, where we can walk and talk in private?"

"Of course."

Santos drove to a park at the southeast corner of town.

It was lush and green with flashes of brilliant flowers showing through the thick foliage. He left his car at the side of the paved road near the wrought-iron gates and motioned for me to follow him.

I walked slowly, admiring what I knew from my upbringing in San Diego was a cordon cactus — the largest type of cactus known in the world. A Boojum tree raised its bare limbs like a four-pronged fork. Cholla crept close to the ground beside the path, ready to grab at my ankles if I made a misstep, and a thorny ocotillo loomed evilly. Around one curve, an elephant tree stood bare and lonely.

"So," I finally said, "who did you talk with at SFPD?"

"An Investigator Larry Kaufman. He speaks highly of you and your work. He told me many surprising facts. Surprising, at least, for a man in my circumstances. You gringas have many more options than most women in my country."

"If only you knew how hard they were won in mine. And how far we still have to go."

"I have an inkling. It was hard enough for

254

me, a man, when I was a student at UCLA."

I'd sensed something different about this law officer from other south-of-the-border cops, and now I understood.

Santos said, "You visited the Smithson woman earlier."

"Yes, I did." I didn't bother to ask him how he knew; it was, after all, a very small town. Possibly he'd put a tail on me.

"Was that where you saw Señor Renshaw?"

"No. He was near the plaza — with Señor Bernardo Ordway."

He nodded slowly. "Did you speak with either of them?"

"No."

"But you did speak with Señora Smithson. What did she tell you?"

"Many things. About Bernardo Ordway, for example. That he's an information gatherer and seller. Judging from his house, he does extremely well at his trade."

Santos smiled thinly. "Better than he has any right to. My government has been after him for years, but he does nothing illegal, such as blackmail. He is like a gossip columnist, only he doesn't print what he finds out. He sells it."

"And since he's only selling what's openly available, he can't be accused of blackmail."

"Technically, no. A case would be very difficult to prove, and my government does not have the resources to pursue it."

"Are private individuals as litigious here as in my country?"

"Most cannot afford to be, and few would contend with someone so powerful as Señor Ordway." Silence as Santos lit yet another of his small cigars.

"Chief Santos, are you aware that Chrysanthus Smithson and her husband were fugitives from justice?"

"Yes. I was not yet a member of the police back then — in fact, I was still in school. By the time I joined, Señor Smithson was dead, and the matter was, as you say it in America, a cold case. From what I have read in the files, they appeared here in the late eighties. American expatriates are common in this country, so few people thought anything of them. They both spoke fluent Spanish, and quickly assimilated into the community. The *señora* found a job tending preschoolers; the *señor*'s health was bad, but he picked up odd jobs when he could. Twice he became ill enough to be hospitalized. Tuberculosis, the *médicos* said. Heart, the *señora* said. The *señora* won the battle of the names, but her husband died anyway, of massive hemorrhages and a heart attack.

He is buried under the big Boojum tree in their yard."

I remembered the tree Chrys and I had sat under earlier, as well as the one we'd passed a few minutes ago. The Boojum, with its warped upright limbs and swollen base, resembles a carrot that has been partially uprooted from the ground. The Suris, indigenous people of Baja Sur, believe that touching this plant will cause strong, often disastrous, winds to blow. Many consider it to be the strangest-looking tree on earth, and — though I haven't viewed all trees extant — I'm inclined to agree with that judgment.

Chief Santos went on with his narrative. "After his father died, the son, Adam, went wild. The gangs, always the street gangs. They patterned themselves after the Crips and the Bloods in Los Angeles, but didn't live up to their *reputaciónes,* and we have had little trouble with them in recent years. One gang member — long since reformed — has told me that Adam boasted of knowing of a place in America where he could get a large amount of money, but no one believed him. Why, they said, if he knew of such a place, didn't he just go take it?"

"Maybe he did. Or maybe circumstances prevented him from doing so."

Santos drew on his cigar. "I think the latter. That is why every time we find unidentified bones dating from the middle nineties, I have them checked against the one dental record we have for him. They are never Adam's."

2:55 p.m.
The plaza was still heavily populated — even now, in the traditional siesta time — when, after we shared a lunch of sopaipillas and Dos Equis, Santos dropped me off. Many of the vendors were packing up their wares and disassembling their makeshift booths, but seemed in no hurry to leave. I checked out the various shops, cantinas, and restaurants, but found no trace of Renshaw. Then I sat at an outdoor table of a café Señora Ibarra had recommended, watching the flow of foot traffic.

I spent the rest of the evening on the phone to Mick and Derek, first asking if Hy had contacted the office (he hadn't), then asking if they'd located Don Macy (negative to that too, but they had a couple of leads they were pursuing). Despite the bad connection — faint with static — we managed to go over various information I wanted them to run down: Ask Emily Parsons if she'd remembered anything more

258

about the Smithsons. Find out who their interim landlord on Clay Street had been. What about the neighbors there? What had happened to the new possessions they'd left behind at Webster Street? The list seemed endless.

I made one more call, and caught up with Craig at home. His contacts at the FBI hadn't known anything about Hy's being summoned to D.C. The news both puzzled and concerned me, but I knew hostage negotiations took time and patience and that the FBI was famously uncommunicative. I'd wait this situation out, as I had many others.

Finally, exhausted, I turned out the lights and fell into a troubled sleep. My dreams were plagued by visions of fire and strange troll-like creatures darting among the flames, and I was half aware of twisting and turning on sweat-drenched sheets. When I woke from one of them shortly before midnight, I decided I'd had enough of Santa Iva, whether Renshaw was still here or not.

■ ■ ■ ■

SATURDAY, OCTOBER 17

■ ■ ■ ■

5:45 p.m.

Getting away from Santa Iva hadn't been as simple or speedy as it had seemed it would be the night before. First I'd had to rouse Enrique and ask him if he would drive me to Santo Ignacio Airport. Then I'd sat around the FBO for hours, unsuccessfully soliciting rides to any point from which I could connect to a commercial flight to San Francisco. Finally, late in the afternoon, a pilot named Steve Millan had agreed to take me to San Diego, but first he'd had to make some phone calls and preflight and refuel, so we didn't get off the ground until the sun was sinking toward the Pacific.

The takeoff was rough, due to a squall that was coming up from the south, and Millan insisted I stay belted into my rear passenger seat, but after we climbed above the turbulence he invited me forward into the cockpit of his Cessna 182 and let me take over the controls. The plane was a sweetheart, flew as if it didn't need a pilot.

"Nice, huh?" Steve said.

"More than nice."

Millan was a personable man, perhaps a few years older than Hy. He had thinning blond hair and the browned and creased face of one who has spent a good deal of time exposed to harsh elements. I'd have recognized him anywhere as a veteran pilot because of his beat-up bomber jacket.

We talked aircraft for a while, and then he said, "I think we may have a friend in common."

"Really? Who?"

"Hy Ripinsky."

"He's my best friend — my husband."

"No kidding!"

"How do you know him?"

". . . From way back when we were doing dirty deals in Southeast Asia."

The casual way he tossed off the comment put me on my guard; I'd had some experience with people who'd been into that scene and they did *not* speak of their activities lightly.

Millan added, "How is the old Ripoffsky?"

The old Ripoffsky. Now that was a tipoffsky.

This man wasn't very bright. No one had

ever called Hy "the old Ripoffsky" — except Renshaw.

"Well," I improvised, "he's still into his Buddhist thing."

"Oh yeah. I never could understand that. What does he do? Sit on a pillow and chant?"

"Mostly he sits in the woods," I said, thinking of Dick Kenyon. "Buddhists are big on nature."

"Glad I'm not one. Bugs, animals, that kind of stuff . . ."

"I'm not big on it either. But if it makes him happy —"

"Sure, why not?" Steve finished for me.

I asked, "Anybody tell you that last year he shaved his head?"

"Because of the Buddhist thing? Yeah, I think somebody mentioned that. Said it looked stupid."

Millan was tangling himself further and further into his lies. If you're going to be untruthful, you should keep it simple. He'd proven he didn't know Hy at all. But he might've been minimally briefed by someone who did — who had hired him to offer me a ride and then do away with me.

I glanced at the flight computer, then down at the verdant stretch of state preserve beneath us. We were beyond the point where we should have turned for the coast. That jungle would be a good place to drop off an unwanted passenger.

I slipped my phone from my purse, quickly checked to see if there was a signal. Relieved that I could get one, I texted my friend Lieutenant Gary Viner on the San Diego police force, asking for information on Millan.

Millan saw what I was doing. "Who the hell you texting?"

"My nephew, to make sure he can pick me up at SFO."

We flew in silence for a few minutes. I could feel Millan building up his nerve. My fingers closed on my .38, still out of sight in my bag. The phone made its little chiming sound as a text came in.

Gary. Millan was wanted for a variety of offenses, including kidnapping and drug smuggling.

I dropped the phone into my lap and grasped the .38 more firmly. Closed my eyes and considered the situation. It was clear that (a) Millan didn't know Hy from an altimeter, (b) Millan was verging on stupidity, (c) Renshaw — probably in collusion with Ordway — had hired Millan to kidnap me. But if Renshaw had ordered a hit, Millan would've pushed me out of the plane long before, above the isolated territory we'd been crossing. Instead we were headed for the coast. Did Renshaw want me delivered alive? And where?

Not SAN, San Diego International — too public, even at this hour. And the ATCs were listening for the faintest hints of trouble in these post-9/11 years. Okay, a non-towered airport in the vicinity, because Millan had said he'd need to refuel at SAN.

I created a mental sectional map.

The county was peppered with airfields public and private, paved, dirt strip, or grass. I'd flown into many, but by no means all, since I'd earned my license.

I checked the flight computer again. We were on direct course to pass over Ocotillo Airstrip, a county-owned facility with two dirt runways, approximately one hundred miles east of San Diego on State Highway 78.

I picked up my phone and auto-dialed Gary's number, saying to Millan, "I'm just going to confirm that my nephew can meet me. He sounded pretty vague in his text." When Gary came on the line, I said loudly to Steve, "We're putting down at Ocotillo Airstrip, runway 927."

He frowned at me. "I thought we were landing at SAN."

"Just put the plane down."

"Why?"

"Because I say so." I showed him my gun.

"What did I do?"

"Try any number of offenses."

"I don't understand!" His voice was becoming panicky.

We were losing altitude too quickly. I corrected for it on the right-seat controls, then said, "You've illegally transported me over an international border. You've been smuggling drugs and what-all for years. Is that enough?"

"Yeah, so? I still don't get why —"

"I omitted the most important thing: you've been taking your orders from Gage Renshaw, and probably Bernardo Ordway."

"You can't prove —"

"Can't I?"

"Who'd you talk to? Ordway would never tell. And Renshaw, he's just a one-time job."

I held out my phone. "You got that, Lieutenant?" I asked.

"Loud and clear — on tape."

Millan's hands and feet left his controls and he wilted back into his seat. I took over and in five minutes I landed the 182 at Ocotillo Airstrip.

Gary Viner and a deputy from the local sheriff's department met us as we pulled off the dirt runway. They boarded the plane and removed Steve Millan, and Viner curtly asked if I'd like to give my statement now or in the morning.

"Gary," I said, "what's wrong?"

His stony expression softened some. "You gave me a scare, Lace Pants." It had been his nickname for me when I was a cheerleader in high school.

"Gary, I'm sorry."

"I just wish you'd give up this dangerous stuff, have a baby or something."

"I think my sisters have done well enough by the world's population without me joining in."

Now he smiled wryly. "My new wife and I too. We're in the process of adopting."

"Good for you."

"About that statement —" he began.

"If I make it now, will you let me sit in on your interrogation of Millan?"

"Sure. I'd say you've earned the right."

Gary had driven his own car. As he drove we talked about the old days: he and John and Joey rebuilding old cars in my parents' driveway; Ma bringing out endless plates of chocolate chip cookies; me hanging around

269

and pestering them to let me tinker with the cars; them telling me to go play with my dolls instead; me bargaining and showing them where Pa kept his secret stash of beer in the garage, in exchange for letting me help tune an engine.

"You staying at the old place?" Gary asked.

"I guess, for the night anyway. D'you ever see John?"

"I run into him sometimes but no, not really."

I sighed, thinking how old friendships fade away. Then I said, "Is it okay for me to make a couple of business calls on my cell?"

"Be my guest."

First I phoned Mick, who had nothing further to report on Hy, Don Macy, or Adam Smithson; then Ted, who told me everything had been fine at the office. And finally I dialed my brother John's number at the family home: no answer; his voice mail said he was off to Hawaii for a "well-earned rest." I almost cried and had started to leave an anguished self-pitying message when a youngish male voice picked up: "Yeah?"

"Matt?" John's eldest.

"You got him."

"It's your . . . aunt Shar." I always felt silly identifying myself that way to either of

John's sons. Both were seven or eight inches taller than me and built like linebackers, and had played semipro football before retiring to join their father in his contracting business, Mr. Paint. Still, it was what they'd called me during their childhoods, and it had stuck.

"Hey, how ya doin'?" Matt asked.

"Okay. How's it with you?"

"Great! Did Dad tell you my big news?"

"I haven't spoken with him for a few weeks." More than that, I thought guiltily.

"Well, Lindsey and me — we're getting married next month."

What a surprise; he'd been going with Lindsey Carlisle since junior high. I was amazed she'd stuck it out with him all this time. "Congratulations!" I exclaimed.

"Thanks. I know everybody's been waiting on us, but I had to get established in the business and save money to buy a house, and Lindsey had things she wanted to do — like that stint in the Peace Corps and the political campaigns."

Lindsey was an activist with a capital *A*. "But now you're settling down?"

"So she says. We bought a nice place in Chula Vista last week and we're even talking about having a kid."

"When's the wedding?" I asked.

"Well, that's the thing. We've got to sandwich it between a world peace conference in Switzerland and a couple of marches in Texas."

"I thought that was all over."

"I've never known the woman to resist a worthy cause, and I can't resist her. When the wedding does come off, are you and Hy gonna be able to make it?"

"We wouldn't miss it. But right now I've got a problem. A cop is about to give me a ride in from Ocotillo Airstrip. Is it okay if I stay at the house tonight?"

"You shouldn't even ask. It's your house as well as ours, you know."

Not really it wasn't, but tonight I appreciated his saying so.

9:47 p.m.

Steve Millan wasn't a problem for Gary or the county investigators; he'd committed his crime in two different countries, and the thought of both the FBI and Mexican authorities moving in on him subdued him and made him contrite. He didn't even bring up the fact that I'd solicited him for an illegal flight, much less that I'd gone with him willingly. As I'd previously observed, he just wasn't very bright. I supposed I should feel some sympathy for him, but if he'd

272

done this now and in the past, what might he do in the future if he wasn't stopped?

"Who hired you?" Gary asked. The other investigators had agreed he should head up the interrogation in spite of his being from a city law-enforcement agency.

"This big man down there — Bernardo Ordway."

"An American?"

"Well, he used to be, but I think he's a Mexican citizen now."

"What were the terms of the job?"

"Five hundred bucks, US."

My life for such a paltry sum? I was offended!

"No," Gary said, "I meant what were you supposed to do with Ms. McCone?"

"Take her to general aviation at SAN and hold her there for a guy named Renshaw."

As I'd expected.

"And then?"

"Turn her over to him and go home."

"Did Mr. Ordway tell you what Mr. Renshaw wanted with her?"

"No."

"You didn't think to ask?"

"Why should I?"

There was a measured silence, then Gary said, "I think we're done here. Ms. McCone, are you willing to file a complaint?"

I balanced the thought of Millan's future conduct against my illegally entering and leaving Mexico with a handgun in my possession. Of putting my license in jeopardy. Rationalized that Millan would be too frightened to repeat his crime.

"No, I'm not."

Gary blinked, then nodded in sudden understanding. "Then we're officially done here. But Mr. Millan, I suggest you speedily exit this jurisdiction."

Millan speedily exited the room.

"Gary," I said, "I want to go home."

11:55 p.m.

Gary was kind enough to drive me "home."

When I stepped into the old house on Mead Avenue, bordering on one of San Diego's finger canyons, the silence nearly overwhelmed me. The rambling place where I had grown up used to ring with the noise of children — too many children, my mother often jokingly complained — but now it was silent as a tomb.

My brother John hardly ever stayed there, Matt had told me; John had a woman friend with a terrific house on Coronado Island, and it had become home for him. Matt was there off and on, but he had a small place near the beach, and his younger brother was in grad school at UCSD and lived close to campus. Ma, twice widowed, had no use for the house, and hadn't for some time; she'd moved away with her second husband, and after he died she'd gotten deeply involved with her oil painting — which was acclaimed in certain circles — and now was living on the Monterey Peninsula. Charlene and her husband Vic, the team of international financiers, spent most of their time in London; their various children had scattered. Patsy, the baby of the family, was managing her third successful restaurant in the Wine Country, with the help of her kids and man of the hour. Joey, sad gentle Joey, had been dead of an overdose for more years than I wanted to remember.

So here was what was left of our childhood. Didn't anybody care but me?

I dropped my bag on the floor, crossed the living room, and opened the sliding doors to the deck. The plants in the hanging baskets and redwood containers were all gone. I remembered Ma taking pleasure in watering them every morning. The lounge chairs were butt-sprung, their cushions torn and dirty. The remains of the vegetable garden — a former swimming pool that sonic booms from the Vietnam-era fighter planes out of NAS Miramar had shattered, and that we'd filled with good dirt and tended with a lot of labor — were long dead.

Nothing lasts. But why did I have to be reminded of it in this cruel way?

■ ■ ■ ■

SUNDAY,
OCTOBER 18

■ ■ ■ ■

9:05 a.m.

I must have fallen asleep on the living room sofa. I knew I'd been crying; there were salty tracks on my face when I rubbed it. The mid-morning sun filtered through the curtains on the doors to the deck, showing how dirty and shabby they'd become. I got up, pulled the offending curtains back, and slid open the doors. The lodgepole pines and bougainvillea in the canyon were competing for height; the pittosporum and junipers were mostly dead. Exotically colored birds soared above, and brought back the memory of the Summer of the Monkey.

The golden lion tamarin whom his keeper at the San Diego Zoo had (for God knows what reason) named Herman was small, weighing less than one pound, and had long, red-gold hair that shone wildly in the sunlight. Apparently Herman didn't like the zoo and escaped to our canyon. Mostly those types of simians live in trees but are very friendly to humans, and Herman's chittering conversation as he made his way from his tree to our back deck had delighted us children.

Then suddenly Herman was gone. Captured and sold to a zoo in Atlanta. The little kids cried. For that matter, so did I . . .

A footstep sounded somewhere inside the house. I reached for my .38, remembered it was tucked into my bag on the front hall table. I braced to defend myself, then relaxed as a soft voice said, "It's just me, Shari."

Nobody but my long-dead father had ever called me Shari. This voice sounded very like his. The footsteps were sure, as if the person knew the house well. Then my brother John's arms enveloped me and I collapsed into them.

"How did you know I was here?" I asked him.

"The McCone grapevine works as well as your people's moccasin telegraph." He was referring to the fact that I am a full-blooded Shoshone, adopted by the McCones soon after birth.

"Oh, shit," I said.

" 'Oh, shit' — why?"

The escaped expletive had been prompted

by John's having shown up a couple of times during my earlier cases and creating havoc by "assisting" me. All had turned out well in the end, but John was better suited to managing his Mr. Paint chain than detecting.

I covered by saying, "The McCone grapevine and the moccasin telegraph are worse than the Internet as far as privacy is concerned. You know what? I think I need a drink."

"Early for one, isn't it?"

"Not really, under the circumstances."

"I think I need one too." He went to the kitchen and soon returned with a tall pair of gin and tonics.

We sat down on the ratty chairs outside; I could feel one of the plastic straps giving way under my weight. I sipped, then said, "I thought you were mainly staying at Anitra's place now."

"I am, but I needed to pick up some documents I have stored here. What's your excuse for coming back to the old homestead?"

Oh no, I wasn't going to get into that! All I'd have to do was mention a case and I'd have a well-meaning but bumbling partner.

I lied, "I had a late-afternoon meeting down here yesterday and most of the flights were jam-packed, so I decided to wait till this morning."

"Why didn't you fly down and back yourself?"

"Seemed like too much trouble at the time."

"Well, what's with that fancy corporation you and Hy founded? They can't pay for a good hotel?"

I shrugged. "Staying here was a nostalgic impulse, I guess."

We looked deeply into one another's eyes. His were gray, mine were black, and both pairs were shifty.

"Liar," he said.

"Liar," I repeated.

After a moment of silence, John stood and went to look out over the canyon.

"Remember the Summer of the Monkey?" he asked.

"I was just thinking of that when you came in."

"I called the zoo in Atlanta a few months ago. Herman's still alive — fat and sassy as ever."

"Whatever made you do that?"

"Was feeling lonely. Anitra left me."

"Oh no, John. Why?"

"Found somebody else."

"So where have you been living?"

"Look around you, baby, this is it."

Not good. Not good at all.

"John, you've made a small fortune from the Mr. Paint franchises. You can afford —"

"Why?"

"What d'you mean — why?"

"What's the good of having someplace nice, when there's nobody to share it with?"

That brought me up short. What *was* the good of it? I'd had the company of my four siblings until I went to college, then roommates and members of the security firm I worked for part time. Even when I'd been working at All Souls I'd spent a lot of time there, in spite of having a tiny studio apartment on Guerrero Street. And then along came Hy who, no matter how long gone nor how far away, is always with me.

Now I flashed on the nights when walking into our empty homes on both Church Street and Avila Street had felt inescapably lonely. . . .

John went to the kitchen for more gin and tonics. I leaned on the railing and said a soft good-bye to the canyon. To the Summer of the Monkey and also to my childhood.

When my brother came back and pressed the drink into my hand, I said, "Is my advice usually dependable?"

"More often than not."

"Then here it is: sell this house and move to one of those swanky condominium towers with three-hundred-and-sixty-degree views. Buy all-new furniture. Clothing too." I eyed his ripped jeans and stained T-shirt disdainfully. "Get a spiffy new car. No more picking up your dates in Mr. Paint trucks."

"What's wrong with a Mr. Paint —"

"And you might consider moving away from San Diego. San Francisco's always been a comfortable fit for me."

John sat, sipped his drink, and set it on a small table — one of the few on the deck that wasn't tipping at a dangerous angle.

"You know," he said, "I've lived down here my whole life, except for those two semesters when I tried college at San Luis Obispo. My business is headquartered here. My boys are here. Some of Charlene and Ricky's kids are right up the freeway in Bel Air."

"I see more of those kids up north than you do down here. They're always visiting their father and Rae. Yours will do the same."

"Ma —"

"Is buried in her art projects in Monterey. Charlene and Vic spend more of their time in London than Bel Air. Patsy's moving closer to San Francisco with every restaurant she opens."

"And Joey's dead."

"Stop that!" I wanted to smack him. "Joey's dead, and Pa's dead, and so are a lot of other people we cared about. But this conversation isn't about dying — it's about living, and living well."

He gulped his drink, stood up, and backed toward the open doors. "I can't talk about this now, Shar. I really can't."

But you will, I thought as I watched him go inside. *You damn well will.*

12:21 p.m.

John has never been one to carry a grudge or even pout for long. His bedroom door opened and shut, then I heard a couple of heavy objects drop to the floor in the entryway. He came out on the deck and said, "You're right. Let's go."

I turned, surprised. "Go where?"

"To my new life."

"San Francisco?"

"Yup."

"Just leave without —"

"Spiffing up the house? Packing up treasures? Having the practically nonexistent mail forwarded? Contacting a real estate agent?"

It made sense — clean break, no time to

sit around contemplating Swiffer mops or Aunt Susan's favorite knickknack. We'd be back to do those things later. Not now.

5:43 p.m.
The smell of grease invaded my nostrils. Cheese and onions too. I struggled up from where I was curled on the car's bucket seat and groaned.

"Come on, Shar," John's voice said. "A burger. French fries. Vanilla milkshake."

They *did* smell good. I sat up all the way. "Where are we?"

"San Luis. I remembered this little stand from when I was in school here. It's just the same."

I ran my hands through my disheveled hair and shook my head to clear it as he unwrapped my meal. God, I was hungry! And the "junk" food, as many would call it, was *good*!

When we'd left John's house, he'd surprised me by opening the garage doors and revealing a beautiful red Jaguar.

"I guess I've already started in on my new life," he said somewhat sheepishly. "I bought it last week."

I'd happily taken over the passenger seat and slept for a few hours. Now, between bites of burger, I asked, "Why'd you want to stop here?"

"Why d'you think? I'm *hungry*!"

My brother was returning to his normal ravenous self. I hoped his new life would continue to agree with him.

8:11 p.m.

My phone buzzed as we sped north toward the Salinas Valley. Mick. For a moment I felt a flash of hope that he was calling with news of Hy.

No. Instead he said, "I've got a line on a guy, Artie Jones, who used to be a friend of Renshaw's. Lives in the East Bay — El Cerrito. I called him, and he's willing to talk with you."

Well, even if it wasn't the news I'd hoped for, it was good.

"I'm about two hours from the city," I said, "maybe two and a half to El Cerrito, depending on traffic. How late is Jones willing to stay up?"

"I'll check. Hold on." He must have had Jones on another line, because he was back within seconds. "Guy says come ahead whenever you can. He's a musician, and he doesn't have a gig tonight."

"Musician, huh?"

"I didn't tell him whose son I am, if that's what you're thinking."

"Good. It might be a bargaining chip for me."

"Jones sounds like he dislikes Renshaw enough that you won't need any chips."

"Okay, tell him I'm on my way. And Mick, I have a surprise for you." I smiled and winked at John.

"A good surprise?"

"One of the best. See you soon."

9:55 p.m.

Traffic was light, even for a Sunday night, and we beat my estimate for our arrival in the city. I directed John to my house and removed my car from the garage, and he replaced it with his. I'd explained about Chelle's staying there and he'd assured me that while he'd only raised boys, he was good at dealing with distressed young women too. I was surprised he didn't insist on immediately getting a piece of my investigation, and I quickly headed for the Bay Bridge.

I'm always wary when crossing that particular span. It's actually two spans, bisected in the middle of the Bay by Yerba Buena Island. Originally constructed in 1936, the bridge has had a troubled history. A fifty-foot section of roadway collapsed during the 1989 Loma Prieta earthquake; extensive seismic retrofitting was done on the western portion, and the eastern portion was totally replaced. Since then faulty and defective rivets have broken, along with crossbars, tension rods, and bolts. All of these problems have caused huge cost overruns and commuter confusion.

But still I drive the bridge. There's also said to be an old statue of a troll — supposedly a symbol of good luck for bridges — on the substructure. But even though I've searched for it with binoculars from a friend's sailboat I've yet to see it. Probably an apocryphal story.

El Cerrito is a small city of some twenty-five thousand that slopes from the Bay shore toward Wildcat Canyon Regional Park. Artie Jones's house was on a cul-de-sac midway uphill above San Pablo Avenue, a main shopping area. The middle of three pink stucco bungalows — Hollywood-style from the thirties or forties, with pitched roofs, dormer windows, and half porches — nestled between two fifties-era apartment houses. All three bungalows were alike, down to their pebbled front yards. Lights glowed softly behind the blinds on the windows of Jones's.

The enormous man who opened the door looked as if he might be from Samoa or one of the other Pacific Islands. His hair was pulled back in a bushy ponytail and his muscular forearms were covered with tattoos. He showed me into a small living room crammed with overstuffed furniture, motioned me to a couch, and flopped down on an armchair across from it. The chair creaked in protest.

"So," Jones said, "you want some dirt on Gage Renshaw? I got plenty."

"How did you come to know him?" I asked.

"His family showed up on the block when I was ten, maybe eleven. We was living down south in Torrance then, my dad worked at the refinery. One day old Gage was there on the streets, and nothing was ever the same."

"How so?"

"Before, us kids all got along. Sure, we had our fights and we was in trouble some of the time, but that was minor stuff, like tagging or slashing tires." He grinned. "One time a bunch of us took on the tires of a Chevy belonged to this old bugger who was always on our backs for making too much noise. Do you know how hard it is to slash a tire?"

"Uh, no."

"Hard enough to make a big guy like me give it up as a career choice. Anyway, Gage was into bigger stuff than that."

"Wait — let's back up a bit. What about Renshaw's family?"

"Father, mother, two brothers — Bob and Pete. Folks're both dead now."

"Are the brothers still around?"

"Bob and Pete — I don't know where they're at, but it's not around here."

Another search to put Mick and his people onto, if necessary.

"Okay, what kinds of bigger stuff was Renshaw into?"

"Started with housebreaking and auto theft. Then he graduated to dealing drugs. Never used them himself, but he got a lot of the kids hooked. Me, I never touched the junk. This body" — he thumped his chest — "ain't no temple of my soul, but I aim to keep it ticking so long as I can."

"Good for you. Was Renshaw ever arrested?"

"Nope. He was cagey — the cops couldn't get nothing to stick. Not even the arson."

"Arson?"

"Yeah. He burned up a neighbor's garage, a paid job, something to do with antiques the guy had stored there and the insurance on them. Cops had both of them dead to rights, but before they could pick Renshaw up, he stole a plane and nobody down

291

there's ever heard from him again."

"He stole a *plane*?"

"Yeah, from a little grass strip out in the country. Crop duster."

"How'd he learn to fly?"

"From the crop duster. Guy helped him get his license and everything. Nice way to repay him, huh?"

"Yeah. This crop duster still around?"

"Nope — died shortly after Renshaw stole the plane. His widow's still alive, though: Mrs. Charley Weeks, at Silver Threads Retirement Home in San Mateo. She sends me a Christmas card every year, because I helped her out with the heavy chores after Charley died."

A good, generous man, this Artie Jones.

■ ■ ■ ■

MONDAY, OCTOBER 19

■ ■ ■ ■

9:30 a.m.

So back I went to the Peninsula. San Mateo seemed asleep on this cheerless, damp October morning. Mist from the sea drifted over the coastal range and showed few signs of dissipating, although, in one of the strange inversions we frequently experience in the Bay Area, the weather in the city had appeared promising.

John had been asleep when I'd gotten home last night and I'd slipped out while he was showering this morning. No acting as my investigative assistant today. With Chelle I wasn't sure what had happened; maybe she'd gone back to her parents'.

From the car I called Silver Threads Retirement Home. Seemed they were well into their day, judging from the perky voice of the woman who answered the phone. Mrs. Weeks? She was in the middle of her

Zumba class. Sure, I could come over and watch.

9:53 a.m.
The woman who admitted me to the exercise room told me the Zumba hour was almost over. I asked about the program, and she said the instructors were licensed by an organization called Zumba Academy. The exercises included music with fast and slow rhythms, as well as resistance training, and the music came from an eclectic assortment of dance styles: salsa, mambo, flamenco, samba, and tango. Mrs. Weeks's Zumba Gold-Toning was a class for older participants with the goal of improving one's muscle strength, posture, mobility, and coordination. And, of course, of socializing.

I could tell that Zumba was working for the women in the class. As near as I could guess, they ranged from ages seventy to eighty-five, and were as supple and coordinated as most people who could claim half their years.

When the session was over, the leader pointed out a slender woman with a pert gray hairdo. She was in avid conversation with another of the participants, and it took me a moment to catch her attention. When she came over to me, I said, "Mrs. Charley

Weeks?"

Her bright-blue eyes blinked at me. "Mrs. Charley Weeks. That brings back memories."

"Why?"

"First of all, call me Rita. I'm widowed, haven't been a 'Mrs.' for a long time. The reason I retained Charley's surname is that it's a damn sight better then Backalulu."

I had to agree with her.

"So who're you?" she asked, using a towel on her damp hair.

I gave her my card and explained what kind of information I was after.

"Gage Renshaw," she said. "That's a name I haven't heard in decades."

"But you do recall him?"

"How could I not recall a man who stole my husband's airplane — and our livelihood? What did he take from you?"

"It's what he plans to take that concerns me."

Rita led me to a table in a small area with vending machines, bought me a cup of coffee. I told her more about Renshaw's past and recent activities.

"Well," she said when I'd finished, "I always knew he was a bad egg. Superficially charming, but with a dark side such as you see in most sociopaths."

Another amateur psychologist, like Gil

Stratton, the FBO owner at San José airport?

Rita added, "I know what I'm speaking of; I used to be a psychiatric nurse."

"What are the indications of a sociopathic personality?"

"It all depends upon the individual you're dealing with. As for the traits I would have assigned to Gage . . ." She paused, refreshing her memory. "Failure to accept responsibility for his own actions, shoving the blame onto others. Many short-term relationships and extreme promiscuity. Manipulativeness, denial, callousness. Pathological lying. And more. In short, all of the characteristics that those of us who are relatively normal don't have or, if we do, manage to control."

"That's one hell of an analysis for someone who must've known him only in passing."

"I'm a quick study where nuts are concerned."

"Have you had any recent contact with Renshaw?"

"Of course not; he's forgotten I ever existed. I hope."

"Was there anyone he was close to when you knew him?"

Again she paused, considering. "He did

have a sort of friend, a man who drove people for a living. Taking people to and from the airstrip, that sort of thing. A tall, heavy, unattractive person — I think Renshaw liked having someone like that around to manipulate so he could shine."

"What was this man's name?"

"It was a long time ago. Let me think." She pressed her fingertips to her brow. "His first name was Don."

"And his last?"

"Macy, I think. Yes, Don Macy. Like the department store."

10:40 a.m.

I drove back up the Peninsula and headed for the office. On the way I worried about having so easily invited my brother into my life. I loved John, and he and I had always gotten along, but I didn't really know him after all these years. Would he be a clingy guest? Demanding? The man who came for a week and stayed seven years? No way of predicting. Had I been too impulsive?

But then I flashed on the sterile, lonely house on the canyon in San Diego: no way he could go on living in such a manner. If there was trouble ahead for us, we'd deal with it.

1:20 p.m.

Traffic was a bitch as I crossed the city. Too many cars, too many people — it had been my driving mantra for years. But here I was, one of them, using up too much fuel, spewing too many fumes into the atmosphere. I'd've ridden a bike, but an old knee injury prevented me from doing so. Taking public transit wasn't really an option in a job like mine, when I might need to leave on a moment's notice, final destination god knew where. So a car was the only solution. Fortunately mine was fuel-efficient and had good emission control, in spite of its image as a rich person's luxury gas-guzzler.

After I'd parked in the M&R underground garage, I bypassed the main lobby by taking the private high-speed elevator to the fourth floor. Early-afternoon quiet there — nobody hanging around chatting, no clients waiting, except for two men in dark-blue vested suits who were flipping through our battered back copies of *Bloomberg Businessweek.* I stopped, eyeing them from a vantage place beside the reception desk.

They looked extremely buttoned down, even for a Monday afternoon in San Francisco: blue-and-gray-striped ties, starched white shirts, highly polished black wing tips. I'm not saying that we who live in the Bay

Area are careless about our appearances, but we do tend to relax some. These men were fully suited up for a power conference. Except for their hair color — one's blond, the other's dark brown — they could have been identical twins, right down to their cleanly shaven faces and manicured fingernails. They reminded me of Craig when he'd put in his first appearance.

FBI. Had to be.

I cleared my throat and the men looked up. "Ms. McCone?" the blond one said.

Yes, he'd been well briefed, probably with photos.

I nodded. "And you are?"

"Special Agent Arthur Kincade, of the Federal Bureau of Investigation. This is my partner, Agent Seth Palmer. Your associate, Mr. Savage, said you'd be coming in and we should wait for you."

So Mick was in the office. Good; that meant he'd turned on the surveillance cams after these two arrived. I studied the IDs the agents extended; they looked genuine.

I said, "What can I do for you?"

"Could we sit down . . . ?" This from Kincade.

"Certainly. Better here than in my private office; it's in chaos and the cleaning staff haven't been in yet."

Kincade nodded and the three of us sat on a cluster of chairs near one of the windows. Palmer crossed his hands on his lap, while Kincade leaned forward, lacing his long fingers between his knees.

"Your husband, Mr. Heino Ripinsky — is it possible he could join us?"

"Not at this time. It's my understanding that you've already been in touch with him."

Kincade widened his eyes and glanced at his partner, who didn't react. So the first agent was going to do all the talking while the other observed. A common interrogative procedure.

"Why would you think that?" he asked me.

"In his last communication with me, several days ago, my husband indicated he was on his way to D.C. at the request of the Bureau."

"I have no information as to that."

"Then why are you here?"

"We understand that you and your husband are connected to a Mr. Gage Renshaw."

Now that was interesting; they'd linked Renshaw to Hy and me. " 'Connected to' isn't the right term."

"What is?"

"Perhaps 'have knowledge of' would be better."

"All right, Ms. McCone. You have knowledge of him. Where is Mr. Renshaw?"

"Why do you want him?" Did it have something to do with Renshaw's — for the want of a better word — vendetta against M&R?

Kincade replied, as if by rote, "That's classified information. Has Mr. Renshaw contacted you recently?"

"What constitutes 'recently'?"

"Just answer the question."

"I can't, until I know what you consider recently."

The men exchanged glances. Kincade said, "Two weeks ago. Exactly."

"That's true, but I don't know where he is now."

"We are recording this conversation, Ms. McCone."

"You should have told me that in the beginning. Under the law —"

"Are you attempting to be obstructive?"

Yes. Because I don't like the sort of adversarial agents the Bureau sends out to conduct these "conversations." Because I don't like your high-handedness. Because I don't like either of you.

But all I said was, "I am not attempting to obstruct anything."

"We want to know about Gage Renshaw.

Where is he?"

"As I said, I don't know."

"This is a federal investigation. Penalties for obstruction are severe."

I was getting angry — unreasonably angry, I supposed — but their smug, stone-faced reactions and replies and now this veiled threat had pushed any number of my buttons.

I didn't respond.

"Ms. McCone, we can take you into custody —"

"On what grounds? I've answered your question truthfully."

Kincade shook his head now, finally showing his frustration.

I said, "Perhaps I could propose a compromise?"

"And what would that be?"

"I don't know where Gage Renshaw is, but I do know where he's recently been. My husband is currently conducting a hostage negotiation for the Bureau. I'd like to know if he is safe."

The agents exchanged glances. Kincade said, "Excuse us for a few moments," and they got up and left the offices.

Kincade returned shortly. "My partner's checking with the Bureau." He sat down and looked at the view. "I've always admired your city, how you've blended the old with the new."

For one whose rage was near the boiling point, I replied civilly enough. "It's taken a great deal of effort, and our planners haven't been fully successful, but we're all learning from our mistakes."

And then we sat in silence. Eventually Agent Palmer returned and handed a slip of paper to Kincade. He read it, then said, "Mr. Ripinsky is safe and will be returning to you shortly. He has been conducting a particularly delicate negotiation for us at a remote location near the Canadian border. No telecommunication has been allowed for fear the hostage takers will pick up on it."

Hy — safe. Even my skeptical nature would not allow me to disbelieve it. The relief I felt was intense.

"Thank you. Thank you both."

They nodded, then Kincade said, "Now, about where Mr. Renshaw has been . . ."

"He visited these offices two weeks ago today. He seemed disturbed, down on his luck, and he couldn't articulate what he wanted from us. My researcher tells me he was last seen in Mexico — Baja California Sur — in a small town called Santa Iva, in the company of a prominent American expatriate, Bernard Ordway."

"Doing what?"

"Connecting with people from his past, I assumed. Renshaw lived a good part of his life in Mexico and South America."

The agents nodded; they knew his story. "And where is he now?" Kincade asked.

"As I said before, *I don't know.*"

The agents continued to question me. When had I last seen Renshaw? Had he tried to contact me? Did he have all my contact numbers? Exactly what had he said when he came to our offices? Then they backtracked: How long had I known Renshaw? Under what circumstances had we met? Had I had any professional dealings with him? Had we gotten on personally at any point?

I answered truthfully, glossing over the fact that we'd first met when I'd tricked him into thinking he was hiring me to kill Hy. I wanted to distance myself from the bastard as much as possible. Finally the agents left, admonishing me to contact them immediately should I have any more contact with Renshaw.

4:40 p.m.

"From what I overheard on the intercom, that was pretty heavy stuff," Mick said after we'd locked ourselves securely within my office.

"Yeah, it was. What do you think about them looking for Renshaw?"

"Frankly, I'm surprised they didn't start long ago."

"Well, his exploits in Latin and Central America would've fallen under the jurisdiction of the CIA, and you know how these agencies are about sharing."

"I hope their interest isn't somehow connected to Hy's disappearance. I mean, you have only those two guys' word that he's tied up in a negotiation."

"I don't suppose you overheard what they were saying when they went into the hall?"

"No, they whispered."

"Or what the one said on the phone?"

"Negative."

I flopped into my desk chair. "Will you get me a drink? Bottom of the bar, single malt Scotch, straight up. A double."

"God, Shar." I don't often dip into the hard liquor in quantity.

"Just to celebrate Hy being safe. And help yourself to the same."

"Will do."

When we were seated, we toasted each other, and he said, "The feds'll make drunks of both of us."

"Hopefully they won't be coming around in the future."

"I've already passed on the info about their visit to Craig and he's pressing his contacts for more information."

"About Don Macy . . ."

"Give me a minute to check with Derek." It was more than a minute before he returned. "We're following up on a lead about Macy possibly working as a chauffeur of some kind, since that was what he did for Tilbury. We've had no luck so far with the usual driver employment places, and Derek's now checking with the ride-sharing firms. Guy's not listed on any of the databases I have access to. I left messages with my sources, but none of them have gotten back to me."

"I guess we're just stuck in a holding pattern here."

We drank deeply. I studied Mick; he looked tired. I'd been loading him up with work, and it was taking its toll.

"So what's the surprise you mentioned to me?" he asked.

"The what? Oh yes. Your uncle's moving to town."

His face lit up. "He's selling the dump in San Diego?"

"It's not a dump, Mick. It's our family home."

"Sorry. I was just a little kid back when I spent any time there."

"I know. And I'm not sorry to see it go. But it's not in any shape to list yet."

"What does Anitra think of the move?"

"That's the bad part — she threw him out."

Mick frowned. Upon the few occasions they'd met, he'd liked John's partner. "Well, it happens," he finally said. "I oughta know, got a history of that. When's John coming up?"

"He's here already, at my house. You might stop by to see him; he's feeling kind of low."

"Will do. I'll take Alison. She can cheer anybody up. If any of my sources calls back with info on Macy, they'll leave messages here as well as on my phones."

5:13 p.m.

After Mick left my office, I went to sit in my armchair under Mr. T. and turned my attention to Don Macy.

Macy had known Renshaw when he drove people to and from the airfield in San José. Recently Renshaw had been here in the city. So the probable scenario was that Gage had looked Macy up and enlisted him in whatever his plan was. And I'd begun to believe that plan was to take Hy and me down. Macy wouldn't have any stake in the plan, of course — he didn't know either of us — so his involvement must have stemmed from whatever compensation Renshaw had offered him. A few hundred dollars? Promises of big money right down the road? Could be either, or something else entirely.

There was a knock on the door, and when I called out, Derek came in. "I've found the firm Macy's affiliated with. It's called YouGo." He handed me a paper he'd written their number on.

"Thanks," I told him. "Good work."

There were several such firms in the city: they connected passengers via cell phone with drivers of for-hire vehicles. Uber, Lyft, and others had come into conflict with the regular taxi companies, who claimed the services were illegal and compromised passenger safety, but the firms had proliferated throughout the United States and Europe.

Suppose, I thought, that Macy had been driving Renshaw, taking him places where he didn't want to be seen, helped him with other activities?

Such as the torching of the Webster Street house?

Renshaw knew about the bonds from Kessell's file. Maybe had known about them for quite some time and consulted the file to verify his information. So why would he have torched the house? And what about Nemo's death?

Nemo . . .

Before I'd thought it merely one of those strange names that contemporary parents saddle their kids with, but now it struck a familiar chord. Something someone had said to me in the last few days had brought it just below the surface of my consciousness.

Think, McCone. Think!

I remembered what Chrys Smithson had said about her son: *He'd pretend he was a character out of a Jules Verne novel, running around in a cape made of bedsheets with a broomstick sword covered in foil, yelling "Ahoy!"*

Nemo was a swashbuckling pirate in Verne's action-adventure books for children. It was natural that a boy who loved ships and the sea as Adam Smithson had would idolize and play at being him. Possible that he'd adopt the pirate's name years later when he wanted to change his identity.

I took out the photograph of the Smithson family on the steps of the Webster Street house. If you looked beyond the young boy's chubby face to the bone structure, he and Nemo could have been identical twins. Or the same person.

But what of it? Nemo had died in the fire. Or had he? He'd been identified only by his dog tags; the autopsy still hadn't been completed — wouldn't be for some time, given the backlog at San Francisco's morgue.

The thought of those dog tags made me wonder why Adam had wanted to become someone else. To escape an overbearing mother? From what I'd seen of Chrys, she certainly had the personality to dominate her son. To free himself of a spotty record with the law? Chief Santos had told me Adam had been headed for more serious trouble than juvenile delinquency. At the time Adam departed Santa Iva, it had been easy to join the military while underage and with a false name. Probably still is; they're always looking for cannon fodder.

One thing bothered me: Why hadn't Adam simply headed for San Francisco, located the bearer bonds, cashed them, and disappeared in whatever way and place he chose? Why wait till recently?

Something had interfered. As much of a loner as he'd been, we might never know what it was. But then again, maybe when we uncovered more of Nemo's history. . . .

No use mulling over that right now. The chief thing was Renshaw. The way to find him was through Macy, so I needed Macy's address and phone number. I called YouGo; they said yes, indeed, Mr. Macy was one of their better drivers.

"I'd like to hire him as a temporary chauffeur," I said to the chirpy-sounding woman on the phone. "It's an extremely confidential job. Is Mr. Macy discreet?"

"Absolutely."

"Before I go ahead with this, I'd like to meet with him in person."

"That can be arranged. Our offices are —"

"Oh no. I couldn't come there. I'm . . . very recognizable. Even my closest aides aren't to be aware of this arrangement."

"I see." Impressed pause; the concept of celebrity overwhelms the average person.

"Is it possible," I asked, "to interview Mr. Macy at his residence?"

Another pause. "How long did you say this job would last?"

"Three weeks, minimum. Maybe longer. I'd expect to pay more than your regular rates, because he'd be on call twenty-four seven."

"Let me check with Mr. Macy and call you back."

"No, I'll call you. As I said earlier, this job is extremely confidential."

6:22 p.m.

When I called YouGo back, I had to go through the same routine as before with the man who was now handling the phones. No, he told me, under no circumstances did they give out drivers' addresses or contact information.

"But the woman I talked with before said she would check with Mr. Macy to see if it would be okay."

"She shouldn't have offered. It's strictly forbidden."

"Even if the job would be long, lucrative, and for an extremely well-known personality?"

"No, I'm sorry." Then he paused. "Wait — would YouGo be granted permission to use this individual's likeness and comments in its publicity if the job turns out to be satisfactory?"

"Of course."

"I'll have to check with my supervisor, Ms. Thomas. One moment please."

When he came back on the line, the man sounded unhappy. "I'm sorry. To quote Ms.

Thomas, 'No, policy is policy, even if the person is a celebrity.' Of course, I do happen to know that Mr. Macy often frequents an establishment on Twelfth Street that caters to off-duty drivers."

7:49 p.m.
I was putting on my coat when John called: "I cleaned out the back of your fridge. What were you trying to grow there?"

"Hey, that was my science project."

"You okay?"

"Tense. Has Hy called, by any chance?"

"Nobody's called. Is there something wrong? Any way I can help?"

"No!" I nearly shouted the word, seeing visions of a bumbling sidekick following me around, then modulated my tone. "You just enjoy your evening."

"They sure ain't what they used to be."

"Don't get maudlin. Order a pizza. Drink some beer. Watch a DVD — we've got hundreds of them. Mick may stop over later with his friend Alison."

"Sounds like a good prescription, Doc. See you later?"

"Yeah — see you later."

So far the day had progressed well enough, but it still could end badly. What, I wondered, was in store for me next? More

315

anxiety over Hy, no matter what the FBI claimed? More taunting from Renshaw? Another near-breakdown on Chelle's part? Further family crisis? Pestilence, fire, flood? An earthquake way up on the Richter scale? And we have live volcanoes near Tufa Lake; were there any that could spew lava as far as the city?

Turned out it was pestilence, in the form of Jill Starkey.

"McCone," she said in her irritating, whiny voice, "just thought I'd warn you — I'm putting out a special midweek edition."

My hackles rose, and I had to fight to control the pitch of my voice. "About what?"

"Incompetence in the city. You and Ripinsky'll be ranked right behind the Muni."

I listened to background noises: people talking, glasses clinking, a TV tuned high to a sportscast. Starkey crunched on what must have been ice and gulped it down.

I said, "I hardly think we rate that high in the grand scheme of things."

"Hell, McCone." Her voice was noticeably slurred now. "You act as if you do."

"Jill, are you drunk?"

"Why shouldn't I be?"

"What's happened?"

"*The Other Shoe* has dropped. I mean,

they dropped it."

"You're not making sense."

"Our backers are cutting us off. This next issue is the last."

If I'd liked her even the smallest bit, I'd have expressed my sympathy, but as it was, I couldn't have been more pleased that her right-wing rag was going belly-up.

"So you, McCone, and your asshole husband are gonna go out in infamy with my paper."

That tore it. "Shut up, Jill." Ah, that felt good!

"That's all you've got to say to me?"

"No. Take this down, record it for your famous last issue, if you're capable in your present state: I'm sick of you, as are a lot of people in the city. You blow up insignificant events for the sake of sensationalism. You slant your stories to suit your own purposes. You take a dislike to people and hound them. You're mean-spirited, homophobic, and otherwise bigoted. You're a lousy journalist, a disgrace to your profession. And what's more, you've got bad hair and worse clothing."

For once Starkey was shocked into silence. She broke the connection with a quiet click.

"Bad hair and worse clothing" was a low blow, I thought, even if it was true. But the

317

rest — right on target.

Starkey would not report my diatribe in print — too much of what I'd said was true — but she'd find another sleazy rag in which to spew her crap, and I'd take a lot of heat from her in the future. No matter, I'd built up a certain reputation in the Bay Area; repeated attacks in a lunatic rag read by the lunatics wouldn't degrade it. So let Starkey shout her message from the rooftops: "McCone's a bitch!"

Sometimes I am.

God, I wished I could talk with Hy! He was always there in my consciousness, as I was in his. Since the beginning we'd had an uncanny connection, a sense of the other no matter how near or far apart we were. I'd know when he was distressed or in trouble, he'd know the same of me. I tried to tap into that now, but it wasn't working. Why not?

And then I remembered what Hy called his "pane of glass": when he wanted to block strong emotions or revelations of pending actions from others, he imagined an insulated, shatterproof glass wall surrounding himself. He was doing that now. And because he was doing so he was protecting me from something it would be harmful for me to know.

But *why*?

Because he knew I'd blunder into the situation and upset whatever delicate balance he'd set up.

I should have realized this days ago . . .

8:07 p.m.
I retrieved my car from the garage and drove to Twelfth Street, to the homey clubhouse in which on-demand drivers could take their breaks and enjoy their downtime. Wi-Fi, big-screen TV, free coffee, camaraderie, food-truck fare, and — very important — restrooms made it an extremely popular stop for those weary of the city streets, and all for only a nominal monthly fee. I showed my ID to an amiable man who seemed to be in charge, and he allowed me to wander among the picnic tables that appeared to be the barnlike structure's chief furnishings.

The first man I spoke with didn't like Don Macy: "Obnoxious little prick, always yapping about his 'high connections.' " He had no idea where Macy lived.

A well-endowed woman avoided him because of his excessive interest in her breasts. "They're big, yeah, but I'm sure he's seen bigger . . . nope, I've never had his address or other information — why would I want it?"

Another woman thought he was "cute — kinda like a puppy dog, only not as yappy." She didn't know the location of his doghouse.

A well-muscled man said, "I offered to help him with building upper-body strength, but that didn't interest him."

And so on and so on: "A loner." "Quiet guy." "Reads a lot in his downtime." "Studies the financial pages in the *Chron,* highlighting stuff with a yellow marker." "Can sit and stare into space for a long time. It gives me the creeps. I mean, what on earth can he be thinking about?"

Great character studies of Macy, but no concrete facts. That is, until I finally reached a bearded man in a heavy woolen shirt at one of the back tables. "Macy? Sure — he's been my neighbor for two or three months. The house was vacant for a long time before that. I mentioned it to Don because I liked the guy and thought we could get together after work and hoist a few beers, but he blew me off, told me to mind my own business." He wrote down the address. "Sorry I don't have his phone number or e-mail, but he never gave them to me."

8:32 p.m.
Don Macy's house was on the eastern slope

of Potrero Hill, not the most desirable of locations there, but situated well above one of the neighborhood's true pockets of squalor. Like many areas in the city, the hill can be described as "evolving" — a euphemistic term encompassing anything from becoming a better class of slum to having the ubiquitous developers throw up luxurious condos to accommodate the techie invasion. When the techies leave for more glamorous quarters, as they inevitably do, the condos will sink down on the scale and the slums will be razed and rebuilt upscale, and the cyclic nature of city life will continue.

No car — it would have been an aged tan Honda Civic, according to information Derek had received from an informant at the DMV — sat in the driveway or anywhere on the street nearby. The house was a corner one, completely dark. It had a small front yard surrounded by a low wrought-iron fence beyond which knobby plants that looked like old rosebushes grew. Although it was hard to make out architectural details in the faint amber-pink light from a nearby street pole, I guessed it was a standard one-floor two-bedroom cottage faced in aluminum siding.

No one home, but that didn't mean Macy

wouldn't return soon. I phoned the office, and my newest operative, Nadya Collins, answered. A former detective on the Santa Cruz force who had taken several years off to raise her twin boys, she'd come to us at the recommendation of the chief down there. She was fifty-two, tall, and strong-bodied, with an engaging smile that I imagined had elicited many a confession from the criminals she'd apprehended. She also possessed a fierce scowl that could fuse a recalcitrant felon to the edge of his or her chair.

I said, "Is there anybody in the office who can run a surveillance on a house on Potrero Hill for me?"

"I'm available."

"Great." I gave her the address and details.

When I finished Nadya said, "Hang on a second. Mick wants to talk to you."

My nephew came on the line. "Craig's just gotten some highly interesting information. He'll be here in fifteen minutes."

"News of Hy?"

"All he said was he wants to see you ASAP."

I made it to the M&R building with two minutes to spare.

"No Craig?" I asked Mick as I burst into my office.

He turned from some papers he was putting in order. "Not yet."

"What's keeping him?"

"Shar —"

"It's bad news, isn't it?"

"He sounded kind of rushed."

"Craig always sounds rushed."

I eased into my desk chair, closed my eyes, distanced myself from the physical world around me. Listened and felt for signals from Hy. There were none.

That goddamn pane of glass! It was still blocking our connection.

After a few moments I moved to one of the sofas, and Mick and I sat silently, waiting for Craig. When he arrived he burst into my office without warning — an unusual move for him.

"Finally got the text of this," he said, and held out a paper. "It's a confidential memo from one of the highly placed ops at the Bureau to a deputy director attached to Homeland Security. It's copied to one of the higher-ups at the CIA."

I stood up, skimmed it, then read it more slowly. It confirmed what the agents who had visited me had said.

"So it really is a serious hostage negotiation," I said.

"Two of them, apparently. In remote areas

where cellular reception isn't good."

"Even if it was good, Hy wouldn't chance making a call that could be intercepted. I've been worried over nothing." After a moment I asked, "What about Renshaw? The Bureau seems very interested in him. Can you find out anything about that?"

"I'll try. In the meantime why don't you think back on your past dealings with him? And remember that what constitutes cause and effect isn't always logical in the mind of a lunatic."

"He wasn't always a lunatic. Something must've pushed him over the edge recently."

"Or he's been over the edge and planning this for a long time."

What Craig said gave me pause. "I understand. But in the meantime what am I supposed to do?"

"As I said before, backtrack on your relationship with Renshaw from now to day one. Get it all noted down. You may figure out what's going on in his twisted brain. At any rate, I'll transmit it to the feds when you're done. And, I hate to say it, but you'll be better off carrying."

Mick asked Craig, "You're advising her to arm herself?"

"Yes, I am."

To me he said, "You told me you were

through with guns."

"I was, but there're some situations that call for extra protective measures." There was no time to explain my philosophy on firearms right now. Especially since it was one of the many issues I still hadn't yet fully figured out.

I added, "I've put Nadya on surveillance at Don Macy's house. Will you please assign somebody to that club on Twelfth Street where the drivers hang out?"

"Will do."

"Thanks. I'll be here in my office if anything comes up. I need to be alone for a while."

Once they had closed the door I sat down at my desk and smoothed out the copy of the memo on top of the blotter. Phrases leaped off the page at me.

Subject has concluded his initial hostage negotiation and has now agreed to undertake a second regarding Code Name Goat.

Subject has conducted a number of similarly delicate negotiations for us, and is eminently qualified. Background on subject:

Subject singlehandedly foiled Project 8879J. Returned stateside and was offered protective custody in return for testifying. Refused and for many years led public life as environmental activist without serious incident.

Subject's wife is well-known private investigator in San Francisco as well as his business partner. Most likely knows of Project 8879J, but not of its significance to present national security. Has had recent contact with our suspect, Code Name Mylar.

Recommendation: Keep Subject in the dark about the Bureau's and his wife's ongoing investigation into Mylar's activities in order for him to concentrate upon this new negotiation. Because of his location at present time, communication between the two of them is highly unlikely.

Good God, I thought, what an inane communication! Code names, such as Goat and Mylar — a type of plastic. Subject. Suspect. Project 8879J. Was this memo written by a real, intelligent person or by a grown-up adolescent running around in tights and a cape?

Project 8879J. Now that sounded real.

Some trace of an old memory associated with it.

Dredge it up. Hunt it down. Get evidence.

I sat for a long time, concentrating. The memory refused to surface.

It must've been something Hy had told me about years before.

When? What? And where was the evidence?

I laced my fingers together, closed my eyes. Tried to remember whatever Hy had told me about that project.

Anything? Yes, I had a vague memory of a conversation we'd had, but I couldn't dredge up any of the details. I'd keep trying till I did.

After a while I went home to bed.

■ ■ ■ ■

TUESDAY,
OCTOBER 20

■ ■ ■ ■

2:25 a.m.

My subconscious disgorged the memory of
the conversation with Hy as I slept, waking
me. Not the details, but I knew where to
find them. I got up, packed a small bag, and
headed for Oakland Airport's North Field.

4:13 a.m.

I lifted off at oh-dark-thirty in Two-Seven-
Tango and set my course due east toward
the high desert country. As the faint early-
morning lights of the Bay Area faded behind
me, I crested the hills at Altamont Pass,
where if it had been daytime and clear I'd've
been able to see the wind turbines rotating
beneath me. By the time I was halfway
across the great agricultural plain beyond,
the fields were taking on definition —
mostly brown of varying shades, inter-
spersed with some green, laid out in neat
squares separated by access roads.

The sky above the eastern mountains was taking on a pinkish-yellow glow. I watched it grow more and more intense before the rim of the sun appeared; after that the fiery ball rose quickly, illuminating the sharp peaks of the Sierra Nevada. At Yosemite I changed course slightly to the northeast, tuning my mike into the chatter on the UNICOM at the small airstrip outside Vernon, by the lake.

"Four-Eight-Seven, that crate of yours sure needs a new paint job."

I smiled, recognizing the voice of a friend, Janie Moore.

"Three-Five-Bravo, I'm surprised you fly that Piper in public."

Another friend, Tim Caxton.

"Break it up, you two," said the bored voice of Amos Tinsdale, who manned the communications shack. "This is an airport, not a playground."

Both snorted.

I said into the microphone, "Tufa Tower, Two-Seven-Tango requests permission to land at your playground."

"Two-Seven-Tango, you're back! About time. Put her down, but watch out for those two school kids up there."

"You got it."

No pretensions or formalities at Tufa

Tower Airport, but it's one of the safest I've ever flown into. Good friends and neighbors look out for each other.

After tying down and spending some time catching up with the folks at the small terminal, I asked Janie Moore, a rangy blonde with a long ponytail, if she would give me a ride out to the ranch and back.

"You leaving so soon?"

"Just a quick trip to pick up some stuff we keep there."

"You guys're never here any more. I don't know how long it's been since we danced at Zelda's or had a fish fry."

I didn't either. "Real life's kind of catching up with Ripinsky and me," I said. "I did tell you in our Christmas card that we merged our companies?"

She nodded, starting her Land Rover. "You're speeding up while the rest of us're slowing down."

There it was: that divide again. How to explain that neither Hy nor I wanted to abandon the things that energized us, gave us purpose and interest in life?

I said, "We'll come up soon, make a party of it. God knows that old house is due for a good cleaning."

And it was. I'd never seen such stupendous cobwebs, such copious rodent droppings, such peeling paint. I went straight to the big bedroom, where there were two brassbound steamer trunks Hy had picked up somewhere years ago. Strained and grunted as I moved the larger trunk away from the wall, broke a fingernail prying loose a panel behind it. The wall safe resided there, some six inches above the baseboard. I'd memorized the combination when Hy had given it to me, long before we were married, but had had little occasion to use it; my important documents were in the safe at the office, and only Hy's old ones were here. He'd shown them to me: deed to the ranch; his and Julie's marriage certificate; her death certificate; a thick file labeled "Chiang Mai." "Feel free to read it," he'd said. "All the details of Project 8879J and my exit from Southeast Asia are set down there."

I'd never read it. I don't know how most couples operate, but Hy and I have a deep respect for one another's privacy. He'd told me many details of his nightmarish years in Asia, but nothing about whatever this project was. And because of that omission, I knew the experience had been extremely painful. If I read about it, he'd feel bound to discuss it, and I didn't want to awaken that pain. He'd seemed grateful at the time that I declined.

But Gage Renshaw had been part of that experience. The file might contain the key to his vendetta.

The papers were inside an old brown water-stained duffel bag. I pulled them out, opened the bag, and peeled off some plastic wrapping to make sure they were the right ones. Yes — 8879J.

When I went back to the main room, Janie was standing at the front window, fingering a deteriorating sheer curtain. "Ramon Perez and his wife want to buy this place, you know."

Ramon and his wife Sara tended the ranch, our horses, and the sheep herd for us.

"He's mentioned it."

"They've done wonderfully with the herd, moved the horses over to be with theirs, where they seem content. And they can afford at least a portion of the property; they've saved their money well."

"What're you saying, Janie?" I asked, although I already knew.

"It might be a kindness to everybody concerned if you and Hy let it go."

She was right, of course. In my haste to get hold of the files, I hadn't given a thought to stopping in to see the Perezes or the

335

horses, King and Sidekick. I hadn't really paid attention to the house, except to notice its shabby condition. I didn't truly believe that we would fly up for a massive cleaning, go dancing at Zelda's, or throw a fish fry.

"I'll speak to Hy about it," I told her. "We'll see."

3:59 p.m.
The stack of files had seemed thicker than I remembered; if I made an immediate return to the Bay Area, I'd be in for a long night reading them and an exhausted, ineffectual morning. But if I stayed here, dirty and dismal as the ranchhouse was, I could squeeze in a few hours' sleep and be somewhat refreshed for the day ahead. So I decided to remain at the ranch overnight to read them, and called Janie to ask if she could take me to the airstrip early tomorrow morning. She readily agreed. "Anytime," she added. "I'm usually up well before dawn. Just give me a holler."

In addition to being filthy, the house was so cold that I made myself a pot of strong coffee and took it and the files to bed, where I turned the electric blanket on high. Half an hour later the sheets were still clammy, but I didn't care. I was immersed in an old story.

Hy's handwriting: **Chiang Mai. The bargain has been sealed. 200 crates of automatic weapons and rocket launchers to be delivered by Renshaw to a private island in the South China Sea, where they'll be distributed within the week to insurgents in two nearby trouble spots. Financial backing of several multinational companies with operations based in the U.S. firmly in place. Guarantee of no governmental interference.**

Whose government? The anonymous countries' — or ours?

Have managed to disrupt Renshaw's plans. He's agitated, uncommunicative, but doesn't appear to suspect me. He can easily be thrown off-balance.

There followed a list of governments, national and multinational companies, and individuals. I sucked in my breath while reading it: a number of US allies; some of the world's most respected firms and prominent citizens. Two members of the US House of Representatives and a senator, now deceased.

Explosive stuff — literally and I can't let it hap-

337

pen. We don't need another Viet Nam.

But I don't want to be stuck in the muck and mire of investigations and congressional hearings. Last week I promised myself I was getting out, getting clean. Going back to the simple life I thought I was bored with but now yearn for. Well, maybe not all the way back because there is no such way, given what I've seen and done here. But a man reaches a point where he can take only so much guilt and recrimination. If there's anything to be salvaged out of this mess I've made, I'll try to find it.

So here's the plan:

Tonight that decrepit old copier in the common room will get a workout after everybody's asleep or out on their flights. Jesus, I hope it doesn't break down. Tomorrow I have a flight scheduled at oh-dark-thirty — more arms for rebels. But the arms are going deep into the South China Sea, and the plane will be ditched well outside US waters. And this original file plus one copy are going with me, to the chopper I've arranged to pick me up.

Renshaw will know what I've done when he sees the original is gone. His plans to gain millions from arms sales will be blown to pieces — blown, another apt phrase — but he'll never be able to come after me, because I have the evidence.

The evidence — where will I take it? CIA, probably. At least, they can have it, so long as they agree to leave me out of it.

I leafed through the rest of the file, nearly choking on my disgust as I read of Renshaw's plans. As I read of how many of the world's most upstanding citizens and institutions had been willing to fund and profit from them.

This was the original, Hy's insurance in case whatever agency into whose hands he had placed the copies reneged on its agreement to keep him out of its investigation. And it had, because nothing about it or its results had ever appeared in the media. Now the FBI wanted control of the case.

One flaw in their thinking: Renshaw was Hy's and mine. We'd be the ones to finally bring him down.

■ ■ ■ ■

WEDNESDAY,
OCTOBER 21

■ ■ ■ ■

4:30 a.m.

It was oh-dark-thirty again when I lifted off from Tufa Tower and set my course for Oakland. I watched the lake and the Sierras recede in the distance and the sun begin to wash over the fuselage as it outpaced me. The Bay Area looked clear, cool, and welcoming.

When I touched down at Oakland, Mick was waiting in my car.

As soon as I'd gotten in, I asked if there had been any communication from Hy or any news about him.

"Nothing," he said, flicking a concerned glance at me. "But we've been keeping on top of everything else, especially Don Macy's whereabouts. He's been going about business as usual — driving, errands, home."

"No slight variation in his routine?"

"Well, a professional driver like him

343

doesn't really have a routine, in the sense of where he goes and with whom. But those new operatives we put on him have logged every passenger and destination. I swear they don't sleep — and unfortunately, they don't let me sleep either, phoning in at all hours."

We were now traveling across the Bay Bridge (my mind, as ever, on those defective bolts) to the M&R building. I asked Mick why he was driving my car, and he described picking it up from my house in a series of automotive maneuverings that astonished me. He hadn't wanted to waste agency money on a taxi. (This from the son of a multimillionaire, who was about to become one himself!) So he'd woken Alison on one of her rare mornings off and prevailed on her to drive him to my house.

Why not take his car or the bike? I asked. Both were in the shop. Then, when he arrived at my house, he'd found John's new Jag blocking the driveway. My brother is neither a willing nor a gracious riser, so for a moment Mick considered hot-wiring the Jag. Fortunately he concluded this wasn't the neighborhood for such early-morning activities. Common sense prevailed further in the person of Chelle, who had seen him and emerged in her bathrobe with John's keys.

My family members are, if nothing else, inventive.

12:05 p.m.
I set things in motion for a staff meeting at four and then, even though I'd caught a couple of hours' sleep at home, napped some more on my office sofa.

The sleep had made me groggy, but I pushed through my mental fog and called Rae.

"No sign of the bastard," she said. "I've canvassed all the data storage places he was hanging around, staked out your building too. Nobody's seen him, and as far as we know, he hasn't had any contact with Macy either."

"I don't think he'd bother to go back to any of those storage companies; he got what he wanted at the Depot."

"Maybe he's still in Mexico."

"No, he got what he wanted there too. Why don't you give it a rest for now and come sit in on our staff meeting? There's been a new development you should know about."

"When's the meeting?"

"Four o'clock."

"I'll be there."

3:55 p.m.
The conference room was ready, with copies of Hy's files placed before each seat. Only Craig had read them, since he was the one operative likely to fully understand FBI-speak. People began to filter in and take their places. When everybody was assembled I began.

"I know I don't have to stress this with you all, but what's said in this room today goes no farther. I trust you to keep strict confidentiality. No exceptions.

"In a way that's too complicated to explain now, I've found out Gage Renshaw's motive for attacking this agency, Hy, and me. There'll be time for you to study the materials in front of you later, so I'll summarize. They concern an illegal overseas arms deal arranged by Renshaw and his late partner Dan Kessell, and thwarted by Hy many years ago. Renshaw's motive is revenge. And his plan for revenge is linked to his search for the three and a half million dollars in bearer bonds supposedly secreted in the abandoned house we were investigating on Webster Street.

"Much of this is theoretical, but I assume Renshaw found out about the bonds somehow and received confirmation that they exist — or existed — while he was in Mexico."

Adah said, "I thought the bonds were destroyed in the fire."

"Maybe not," I told her. "As you remember, I saw someone running away from the house immediately before the fire flared up."

"Renshaw?"

"Could've been. The man was Renshaw's height and body type."

"Macy's too. It could've been him, acting on Renshaw's orders."

"That's also possible."

"What about the man who was killed in the fire?"

"Nemo James, Michelle Curley's boyfriend. I haven't confirmed this yet — and maybe no one ever will, since he was very badly burned — but I believe his true identity was Adam Smithson, son of the man who stole the bonds. I have a photo of James as a boy, but I only saw him in the flesh as an adult in his thirties. After studying the photo and showing it to Chelle, I've concluded there's a similarity in facial bone structure that an expert will probably confirm. There're also incidents in his childhood that indicate why he would adopt the Nemo alias."

Derek asked, "Was he after the bonds too?"

"Yes. He knew about them from his father, who died before he could go back for them."

"Why'd the son wait so long to try to retrieve them?"

"I know," Mick said. "It occurred to me last night, and I checked with the state board of corrections today. Smithson was in prison all those years under his own name for an armed robbery he committed in San Diego. The personal history he presented to Chelle is an outright pack of lies."

Julia said, "So this Nemo guy was looking for the bonds and along came Renshaw, who was also looking for them. The timing's quite a coincidence."

"Coincidences *do* happen," I said, "sometimes in bunches — otherwise there wouldn't be any such word."

"True. So Renshaw bumps him off or otherwise disables him and gets the bonds and sets the house on fire. Deliberately?"

"No way of knowing. Until we get hold of Renshaw."

"We?"

"Yes — we."

"Tall order."

Adah asked, "These bonds — can they still be redeemed?"

I glanced at Derek, who was keeping in touch with various financial institutions.

He said, "Yes, but I just found out today that the date they expire is coming up next month — another reason Nemo may have been anxious to get hold of them."

"And have any of them been redeemed since the fire?"

"Not yet. Renshaw's probably made some illicit arrangements for cashing them, but hasn't had the opportunity to act on them so far."

I thought of Señor Bernardo Ordway. Now there was a man who would know what to do — for a steep fee. That had probably been Renshaw's reason for going to Mexico.

We talked some more, going round and round on the same issues: Did Renshaw have any accomplices? Was he as truly unbalanced as we thought? How had he managed to function all those years if he was? What was the trigger that had pushed him into action against Hy and me?

During this session my phone rang: Nadya Collins, the relatively new operative who was tailing Macy. I left the conference room and took the call in the hallway: Macy had gone to Safeway after getting off work, and somehow she'd lost him there. "It's a big store," she added apologetically. "He disappeared in the produce department, and when I came out his car wasn't in the parking lot. I drove over to his house, but it wasn't there either and the place is totally dark."

"Continue your surveillance of the house for the next twenty minutes or so, and then I'll take it from there," I told her.

Action was what I craved, not more brainstorming. My best lead to Renshaw was Don Macy, and the place to intercept Macy tonight was at his home . . . if he finally came home. I wanted to be the one to do that.

6:21 p.m.
Nadya was parked a short way downhill from Macy's rented house. I pulled up behind her gray sedan and flashed my lights to let her know I'd arrived, which was our prearranged signal. She left immediately.

I took my .38 from my purse, where it had been since before I flew to Tufa Lake, and slipped it under the waistband of my jeans at the small of my back. Then I stuffed the purse under the seat and got out of the car. The night air was balmy, as it often is in September and October, San Francisco's true summer months.

I climbed the short front steps of Macy's home and pressed the bell. I didn't expect an answer and I didn't get one. I moved along the driveway, looking for signs of recent habitation, but there was nothing to see. The blinds and curtains were all tightly drawn. The driveway ended at a cracked concrete pad where a garage or carport might once have stood; it was so deep in the shadows that I hadn't noticed it before. I took out my small flashlight and shone it around, shielding the beam with my other hand. Oil stains, some old, some newer. Rotted foundation posts from an old super-structure surrounded the concrete.

I returned to my car, made a U-turn, and parked a few houses down on the opposite side of the block. Adjusted my side-view mirror so I had a good view of the Macy house. Below, the city thrummed to its own distinctive beat: the faint roar of freeway traffic; people calling their children and pets inside; music of various sorts. Brakes screeched, horns blared, sirens wailed. Life was going on down there, and here I sat with what so far was a dead-end case.

Most people don't understand that a lot of a private investigator's work involves dead ends: A promising lead turns up and you follow it doggedly, but it takes you nowhere.

You sit in your car, run out of food and water. Or you bring too much water and end up having to pee in ludicrous places. You park facing the wrong way, and the subject sneaks around you easily, but you don't realize he or she has gotten away till the next morning. You're bored out of your mind, your butt aches, but you don't dare get out and exercise or play a DVD. You attempt to fantasize, but if your dreams involve what you used to do in the backseat of a decades-old Chevy, they're pretty hard to fit into the front seat, even of a brand-new luxury car.

God, the night was black! I didn't often conduct surveillances any more, and it had been a while since I'd had to contend with such dark, lonely places. I flashed back to a long-ago confrontation on the US-Mexican border south of San Diego, where I'd had to kill a man. That had been one of the darkest nights I'd ever experienced, but I'd felt strong. Last night at the ranch, when I'd taken a short break from reading Hy's journal to walk in our meadow and looked up at the stars over the high desert, I'd felt a measure of comfort. When I'd made my first night flight, the sky had been black, with clouds scudding across it, and it had welcomed a fledgling pilot. But here, with the lights of the city fanning out below, the night felt impenetrable, and I felt profoundly alone.

A few cars passed, but none of them stopped. A motorcycle buzzed by, its driver trailing a long white scarf. A man walked a blond lab, but displayed no interest in me. A shabby pickup truck rattled past. I felt like I was like a computer in sleep mode: waiting, waiting, waiting . . .

10:02 p.m.

After a while I broke one of my own rules and got out of the car and took a walk along the block. It sloped sharply to the south, then rose to another precipitous height. All the time I kept my gaze on the Macy house. A couple of cars passed, but neither turned into Macy's driveway.

Was Macy coming home, or had he perhaps gone to meet Renshaw in another part of the city or even someplace farther away after shopping at the Mission Street Safeway? My assumption was that he'd been doing his grocery shopping and then would head for home. But he hadn't. . . .

Until now. Finally.

I watched as Macy's Honda edged into his driveway and parked far back on the concrete pad. I couldn't see whoever got out, but after a moment a man's figure appeared, lugging a couple of bags to a side entrance.

After some fumbling with keys, he went into the house. I watched as a light came on behind closed blinds in a room I supposed, by the number of exhaust pipes in the roof above it, was the kitchen. After a few seconds the light went out, leaving the place as deserted-looking as before. He hadn't bothered to put away his purchases. Or to turn on any more lights.

Why? What was he doing in the dark?

When I came home to my empty house late at night, what did I do? Turn on lights and leave them on until I'd made sure everything was secure, even though I have a good alarm system. I'd check for messages, maybe take a look at the TV news in case I'd missed one of our all-too-frequent catastrophes. I'd use the bathroom, brush my teeth, sometimes take a shower.

Maybe I was overly fastidious.

Maybe Macy was drunk or careless.

Or maybe he'd spotted me and hoped I'd go away.

The hell with that!

I crossed the empty, echoing street. Went up to Macy's door and rang the bell, keeping my thumb on the button.

It took more than a minute for the door to open. Macy looked out at me with owlish eyes.

"Mr. Macy, I'm Sharon McCone, a private investigator. I need to talk with you."

"At this time of night? About what?"

"Gage Renshaw, among other things."

"Who?"

"Come on, Macy. Your friendship with Renshaw is well documented."

"Friendship? What're you talking about?" Beads of sweat stood out on Macy's high forehead now. His eyes jerked to his left.

I glanced that way, but saw nothing in the darkness behind him. "What are you so afraid of?" I demanded.

"Afraid? I'm not afraid of anything. You're bothering me late at night, invading my privacy —"

"Tell me about Renshaw and I'll go away."

"I can't!"

"You can, and you will."

I moved forward, putting my left hand on the partially open door. Macy braced it against me. I pushed it, and suddenly the resistance eased. Macy's mouth popped open in surprise. A hand came out of the darkness, gripped my upper arm, and dragged me into the foyer.

A familiar raspy voice said, "I'll take care

of her, Don."

Renshaw.

The son of a bitch had been in the house the whole time.

11:20 p.m.

I tried to wrench away, angry with myself for having been caught off guard this way. The anger gave me strength and I almost broke his grasp. He tightened it, jerked me around, and slammed me face-forward into the foyer wall. At the same time I heard him growl at Macy to turn on the light, to shut and lock the door.

Macy did as he was told. I struggled in the sudden brightness, but Renshaw had me pinned with one hand and the weight of his body. "Well, what have we here?" he said, and I felt him reach under the hem of my short jacket and pull my .38 from the waistband of my pants. Then he released me, stepped back. I turned away from the wall to face him.

He stood with his feet planted, holding my gun in one hand and a small-caliber automatic in the other. Two-gun Renshaw. My stomach muscles clenched, and not only because both weapons were pointed at me.

God, he was a caricature of his former self. Once perfectly groomed, he now smelled of stale sweat, of tobacco, of fried food, of generally bad hygiene. Two buttons were missing from his plaid shirt, and in between I could see tufts of matted gray-black chest hair. His eyes, which had always been keenly intelligent, bulged and blazed with a maniacal light, their whites threaded with broken blood vessels. Yellowed teeth showed through a self-satisfied smirk.

"Gage . . ." Macy's voice was a nervous squeak. He was afraid of Renshaw, and with good cause.

"Shut up, Don. Go turn on the light in the living room."

Macy immediately hurried through an archway to our right. Light bloomed in the room beyond.

"All right. Now go get the bracelets from my bag."

Bracelets?

"Why, Gage? What're you —"

"Don't ask questions. Just do it!"

The burly man bobbed his head, disappeared into the rear of the house.

"Surprised to see me, huh, McCone?" Renshaw said.

I didn't reply.

"Didn't figure I was here, did you? No better place to hole up the past few days with my computer, get everything set on my big deal."

Sitting in the dark like an animal in a cave. He really has gone around the bend.

"Well, I'm glad you showed up," he went on. "Saves me the trouble of having to go hunting for you."

I didn't give him the satisfaction of an answer.

"What's the matter, McCone? Cat got your tongue?"

Fuck you, Gage.

He chuckled, then gestured with my .38. "Into the living room. Go on, move."

I moved. The living room was a pack rat's lair, crammed with mismatched and haphazardly arranged furniture and miscellaneous objects: here a rusted lawn mower, there a shopping cart filled with baled newspapers; here an old thick-bodied TV set on a sagging metal stand, there a cardboard carton overflowing with empty bottles. Books, both hardcover and paperback, spilled over the floor. Rolled rugs leaned against one wall, a large cracked baroque mirror beside them.

Macy came back down the hallway, stopped next to Renshaw.

Renshaw said to me, "Hold it right there. Take off your jacket and drop it on the floor."

I obeyed.

"Macy, check it for a weapon."

Macy scuttled forward, picked up the jacket, and shook it. My car keys fell out, and he snatched them up and pocketed them.

Renshaw motioned with my gun. "Turn all the way around. Arms out. Slow."

I did that too. I was wearing a bulky sweater with no pockets and a pair of jeans. He could plainly see that I wasn't carrying any other weapon.

"Now go over to the fireplace. Stand with your back to it."

The fireplace was one of those small ornamental ones you find in old houses like this, carved with the kind of curlicues and flowers and cherubs' smiling faces that had adorned many a Victorian parlor. Along both sides were long, slender vertical posts of marble cemented into the brick facing.

"Go ahead, Don, cuff her to one of those posts."

A jangling sound. Christ. Now I knew what Renshaw had meant by bracelets.

Macy moved over beside me, snapped one cuff around my right wrist and the other around the marble post.

"Search her," Renshaw said. "See what she's got in her pockets."

Nervously Macy patted me down. I stood

stiffly, submitting to it with my jaw clenched.

"Nothing, Gage."

No, not a damn thing. My purse was locked in the car.

"Okay, Don. Now you get out of here, go wait in the kitchen while I have a little time alone with our guest."

"But the appointment . . . we've got to leave pretty soon."

"I know it. Just do what I told you. This won't take long."

Macy went away again.

"Well, McCone? Anything to say now?"

No.

"Don't you want to know about my deal? Sure you do. It's big, the biggest one I've ever pulled off, thanks to those bearer bonds."

He had lowered his voice into a confessional mode. He was going to tell me his whole story to feed his out-of-control ego. Of course it didn't matter to him what he revealed, because he intended to kill me.

"You know about the bonds being in the old house on Webster Street, right? Bernardo Ordway in Santa Iva told me they might still be there. He's been peddling information to me for years; has quite a cottage — pardon me, hacienda business going for himself. He said those bonds were a kind of family folklore with the Smithsons; their nerdy son ran away years ago, got put in prison for something he pulled in San Diego. But as soon as he got out he hurried up here to look for them. He'd been sniffing around the house for quite a while before I sent Macy there to see what he was doing. Too bad for him he ran into Don."

Macy. So it was Macy, not Renshaw, I saw running away from the burning house.

The crazy light grew brighter in his eyes. "Aha! You figured it was me you chased that night, huh? Me who killed the Smithson guy. You should've known better, McCone. I wouldn't've panicked like Macy did, knocked the guy out, and then torched the place. No need for all that."

He was right, I should have known better. Renshaw never did his own dirty work when he could find someone else to do it for him.

"Not that it matters now," he went on. "All that matters is that I got the bonds. Ordway brokered them for me down in Mexico. Half the face value, a million five in cash, less Ordway's commission. Tonight's when I collect from Ordway's representative. That's what Don was doing before he got here, setting up the meet. We'll go in his car with me on the floor in back, just to

361

be safe. Jesus, I'll be glad to get out of this crappy house full of junk and mouse shit. It ought to be condemned."

I stood as still as the marble I was cuffed to. He was in the mood to gloat, as many megalomaniacs do, and he'd lost all sense of logic, perspective. He didn't need any comment or prompting from me, but I asked, "What're you going to do with the money, Gage?"

"What do you think I'm going to do with it?"

"Live luxuriously, I suppose."

"More than that. I've already hired myself a hacker, guy named Maloof, better than that boy wonder of yours, the best money can buy. He's pulling up everything in M&R's files, a lot of other people's confidential files as well. Info on all sorts of nasty secrets that people in this country'll be grateful to pay to keep covered up."

So that's your bottom line. But what you don't know, you crazy bastard, is that M&R has the details of your failed arms deal and the FBI's warrant on you. And we took care never to enter a word of those files into our computer system.

"Well? What do you think?"

I didn't reply.

His mouth tightened with anger. Men like

362

Renshaw don't like to be stonewalled. He'd once been the unflappable partner at RKI, bringing calm to highly charged situations, dealing smoothly with panicky clients. But that was the old Gage. This nutjob was the exact opposite, as volatile and deadly as a stick of dynamite with a lighted fuse.

"I could kill you right now," he snarled, "only I'm not going to. You think you're such a goddamn ice maiden, but you'll sweat plenty before I'm done with you. So will that bastard you're married to, because he won't know if you're alive or dead until I get good and ready to tell him."

"Why?" I asked.

"Why what?"

"Why do you want me dead and Hy to suffer? What did we ever do to you?"

"What did you do? Jesus! Years ago Ripinsky screwed up a major deal for me in Southeast Asia. Then when the two of you merged your companies you made absolutely no effort to find me, bring me back into the fold. And when I came back from south of the border and looked you up, still no offer to compensate me for my rightful share. Instead you've been scrambling to get rid of me, get something on me that'll make it impossible to claim my share."

His share! My God! As if he were entitled to

anything from us!

"Gage, in the first place, after you disappeared we thought you were dead. You left without a word —"

"You *hoped* I was dead. You two smart operators and your crack team of investigators could've found me easily enough if you'd tried. But no, Gage was gone and you rejoiced in it. Well, now it's my turn to rejoice. And that's just what I plan to do."

Macy appeared in the archway. "Gage, it's almost midnight."

"Yeah, all right." Renshaw backed away, paused, then held up my .38 and smiled slyly. "Nice little piece you've got here, McCone. Know what I'm going to do with it?"

I shook my head.

"Just watch." He crossed the room to where a large, clear glass vase sat atop a file cabinet a dozen feet from me and dropped the gun inside it. "Right where you can see it the whole time you're waiting for us to come back."

He laughed, went to join Macy. "Yell your head off," he said to me then. "There's nobody close enough to hear you. Struggle all you want, tear your wrist to bloody shreds, but I guarantee you won't get free." He laughed again, and then the two of them were gone.

As soon as I heard the sound of Macy's car pulling out of the driveway, I slid the cuff on my bound wrist up and down the support post from top to bottom. Marble has a reputation for solidity, but actually it cracks easily enough if you can find a flaw in it.

But there was no flaw in this piece. No cracks, no chips, not even a hairline fracture.

The cuffs themselves had a cheap look, as if they'd been bought at a surplus equipment store. I ought to be able to pick the lock if I could find something to use, or to wrench the mechanism loose by continually pulling and yanking on it.

Wrenching didn't work.

Renshaw had been right: I couldn't get free.

■ ■ ■ ■

THURSDAY,
OCTOBER 22

■ ■ ■ ■

1:05 a.m.

Oddly enough, through all this time and chaos, my watch had not stopped. Its luminous dial reminded me that the window of time before Renshaw and Macy returned was growing smaller by the minute. I had to get loose.

But how? How?

My wrist was already bloody from all the futile yanking and twisting I'd done over the past hour. No escape that way. I had nothing I could use to pick the handcuff lock. My jeans were of the stretchy zipperless style, so I couldn't even use the pull tab. And my boots were also pull-ons, with low square heels.

If only there were some heavy object within reach that I could use to smash the marble post. Only there wasn't. The closest pieces of furniture were an overstuffed chair to one side of the fireplace and an old scratched-up credenza on the other. Sitting on the hearthstones, as I was now, I could reach the credenza by stretching out my leg, but it was too heavy to move and there was nothing on it I could dislodge that might be of use.

For the dozenth time my eyes roamed over the room, avoiding my .38 in the big glass vase on the file cabinet. Damn Renshaw. The nearness of the gun was the torment he'd intended it to be.

Stapler on the arm of the overstuffed chair. Could I stretch out far enough to reach it? No. And even if I could have, the stapler didn't look heavy enough to break the marble.

The only other possibility was that floor lamp in front of the credenza. I hadn't been able to reach that either, but I had nothing to lose by trying again. It was one of those old, heavy metal ones with a faux onyx base and legs like little lion's paws, and a stained glass shade. If I could manage to bring it down and break the shade, maybe I could use a shard somehow. . . .

I wriggled around on the hearthstones, pulling, stretching body and legs. Still couldn't quite reach the lamp. By all but tearing my arm out of its socket, I managed to gain the necessary inch for my flattened foot to touch the base. The lamp teetered slightly, then stood pat.

I hated those lamps! There had been one next to the keyboard in my piano teacher's house the year my parents cajoled me into taking lessons. I hated those lamps almost as much as I hated pianos —

No tangents, dammit.

I stretched out again, until the pain in my wrist and shoulder became unbearable. My foot touched the base again, but all it did was wobble the lamp and nudge it away from me. The damned thing remained erect and now was completely out of reach.

Shit! Now I *really* hated lamps like that!

I wiggled backward to ease the strain on my wrist, arm, and shoulder. Sat up with my back against the fireplace next to the post. Blood trickled down from my torn wrist; I could feel it wet and warm inside the sleeve of my sweater. My whole body ached from exertion, frustration, the sharpening edge of panic.

Car outside. I held my breath. It went by without stopping, its tires swooshing on the pavement. Had it been raining?

Concentrate. Focus.

Focus on what? There was nothing nearby now but dust balls beneath the credenza —

Wait a minute. Was that a glint of metal

under there that I hadn't noticed before?

I bent forward as low as I could for a better look. Glint of metal, yes. Metal and wood.

Mousetrap!

My pulse rate jumped. That was exactly what I needed, didn't matter whether it was set or unset or held a squashed rodent. If I could just reach far enough with my foot to slide it out . . .

I scrunched down again on the hearth, extended my leg, flattened my foot as much as I could. The space under the credenza was narrow, and at first I thought I wasn't going to get my foot under it. I kicked off my boot and tried again.

This time I was able to squeeze my toes underneath. But I still couldn't reach far enough to touch the trap. The edge of the credenza bottom bit into my instep, scraped painfully. I gritted my teeth and kept struggling, gaining a fraction of an inch with each forward push —

There! My big toe touched the trap.

I managed to ease it up, hold it in place. Then, slowly, I drew it back toward me.

My toe slipped off. Damn! Carefully I lifted it into another hold and again slowly eased the trap backward. It wasn't set, or if it was, the movement didn't release the spring. The last thing I needed was to have it snap down and crush my toe.

Now I was able to get two toes onto it, a third. That made moving it easier. I managed to draw it out far enough that the credenza edge was no longer scraping my foot. Then I was able to pull with all five toes.

Once I had it into the open I saw that it was an old-fashioned kind with a slender metal lever used to set the spring. Good! I dragged it as close to me as I could, twisted my body until I was able to reach it with my free hand. It must have been under the credenza a long time. Not only was it caked with dust, it contained a tiny mouse skeleton.

My free hand was shaky from the strain. I willed it steady, then anchored the trap with my foot and lifted the spring mechanism far enough to dislodge the skeleton. The trap was ancient, the metal corroded, but dismantling it one-handed seemed to take forever. I was oiled with sweat when I finally wrenched the lever free.

I pulled myself up until I was leaning back against the fireplace next to the marble post. Then, using the lever as a pick, I went to work on the lock of the handcuff circling my wrist.

I'd been at it for less than a minute when I heard the sound of another car approaching outside. But this one didn't pass by — it pulled into the driveway, onto the concrete slab.

Jesus! Renshaw and Macy were back.

Frantically I dug at the handcuff lock.

A door banged open at the rear of the house. I heard the mumble of voices, then distinct words.

Renshaw, his voice furious: . . . fucking Ordway's not gonna get away with screwing me!

Macy: Maybe he didn't. Maybe it was the guy who was supposed to deliver the money —

Renshaw: A double cross in any case. Ordway's gonna pay one way or another.

Macy: Gage, you're not thinking of going back to Mexico —

Renshaw: The hell I'm not! I need a drink. Shut up and pour me one.

Come on, dammit, release! Release!

Macy: What about McCone?

Renshaw: What about her? That part of it hasn't changed any.

Macy: Hadn't we better check on her?

Renshaw: What for? She hasn't gone anywhere.

Come on, come on, come on!

Macy: Gage . . . you're not going to kill her here?

Renshaw: No, not here.

Macy: Where, then? When?

Renshaw: Never mind that. I need a drink. Shut up and pour me one. Then we'll deal with McCone.

Got it!

The lock snapped and the steel staple was loose. I yanked it out, freed my wrist. Lowered the cuffs to the hearth to keep them from jangling. Put on the boot I'd kicked off. Crossed the room as fast and silently as I could.

Out in the kitchen I heard the clink of glass on glass.

My legs were wobbly; one of them gave out just as I reached the file cabinet. I couldn't stop myself from staggering against it. Off balance, I went down on my right knee — the one I'd injured a few years before. Up top the vase teetered, toppled. I grabbed for it as it fell, but it slipped out of

375

my blood-slick fingers and crashed to the floor.

Shouts from the kitchen.

I lunged for the .38, caught hold of it, dragged it from the shards of broken glass. Straightened and assumed my shooter's stance just as Renshaw and Macy came charging in.

"Hold it right there, both of you! Hands up!"

They skidded to a stop. Macy squeaked, "Christ, she's loose!" and then froze. But not Renshaw. His mouth twisted, his face congested with fury, and he clawed for the automatic shoved into his belt.

I remained with my legs spread, .38 held in both hands at arm's length. "Don't do it, Gage!"

"Fucking bitch! Not gonna let you stop me now!"

He pulled the automatic free, started to bring it up.

I fired a second before he did.

His shot went wild, the bullet smacking into the ceiling. My shot didn't. It nailed him high on the right side of the chest, jerked him half around and made him lose his grip on the automatic. His knees buckled and he went down. Flopped over, grunting, against the ornate Victorian baseboard.

I moved quickly, kicked the gun out of his reach. Macy was cringing against the archway wall, both hands as high in the air as he could reach. "Don't shoot me, I'm not armed, don't shoot!"

Renshaw tried to get up, but couldn't make it. He lay there clutching at his bloody chest, glaring hatred and spitting obscenities. Lucky for the crazy bastard I hadn't aimed a couple of inches closer to his heart.

Lucky for me too. I didn't want another death on my conscience, not even Gage Renshaw's.

■ ■ ■ ■

FRIDAY,
OCTOBER 23

■ ■ ■ ■

9:17 p.m.

A busy day had passed since I'd escaped Renshaw's clutches. Now, finally, I was in my living room waiting for a call from Hy and talking with John about his new housing. He had a sheaf of brochures that contained floor plans and descriptions of the condos in the new high-rise in SOMA where he'd decided to buy.

"I kind of like the three-bedroom unit with the Bay-view balcony," he said. "Plank floors. Appliances by some classy European company I've never heard of. Granite slab countertops. Ample space for outdoor barbecuing. Walk-in closets. I could save a bedroom for guests and turn the other into a home office. I'd need rugs, though — I hate to walk on bare floors when I get up in the morning. Blinds. All kinds of furniture. And color schemes. D'you think I'd need a decorator?"

This from a man who, till recently, had been holing up in the deteriorating family home.

I pulled one of sister Patsy's quilts over me and stared into the guttering fire. "Buy the condo, John," I said.

"You really think I should?"

"Rooftop pool and tennis courts? Health club? Deluxe catering from two Zagat-recommended restaurants on the ground floor, that offer in-home dining? What's not to like?"

"It's awfully upscale. Ma would call it snooty and selfish."

"Yeah, until she visited and you ordered up the first Zagatrated dinner for her."

"I don't know . . . maybe it *is* kind of self-ish."

"So volunteer for a charity. Become a Big Brother — you're good at that. Use your surplus income to do some good."

"I could, couldn't I? I'd like being a Big Brother — I've done it again and again."

"Go for it, John. And now shut up because my phone's ringing."

Hy was at JFK, waiting for his flight home to SFO. "How're things there?" he asked.

I related the story of my ordeal with Ren-shaw, omitting some of the more unpleasant details.

His voice shook when he said, "That was a pretty narrow escape you had."

It was the first time I'd been able to talk with him since it happened. In all the chaos of the past day we'd missed connecting with one another several times. The happiness I now felt at the sound of his voice was immeasurable. "Yeah, it was bad, but it's over."

"McCone, I thought you and I were supposed to preside over M&R like elder statespersons, and let the others take the risks."

"So did I, but you know what? Elder statesperson isn't what either of us is cut out to be."

"No, it isn't. No elder statesperson could be as pissed as I am at the FBI without succumbing to a heart attack. The second hostage negotiation was critically important, yes, but they shouldn't have kept me in the dark about what was happening with you and Renshaw. Personally I think they wanted to nab him themselves and grab all the glory. They underestimated you."

I sat down at our kitchen table and covered my other ear, blocking out the drone of a football game John had turned on in the living room. "What *was* all that nonsense about them sending a plane to Miami to take you to D.C.?"

"Initially it was intended to confuse the hostage takers in case they intercepted any communications and found out I was on my way. Which, of course, was totally ridiculous because the guys who took the woman hostage in upstate New York didn't know me from Barack Obama."

"These guys — can you talk about them?"

"Not on an open line. And they're not particularly interesting. Just a couple of not-very-bright pseudo-patriots who thought they could save the country by holding the local school superintendent until their demands were met. The second negotiation — the senatorial candidate — was much more serious. I'll tell you about that when we're together. But Renshaw — what's his status?"

"He's recovering under guard at SF General from the superficial chest wound I inflicted on him. He's gone completely mental. Keeps ranting about wanting his money. He earned it legitimately, and Ordway is just holding it for him. Macy's a buddy from way back who loaned him a room in his house while he was waiting for Ordway to deliver the cash. He's going to sue — me, you, the City and County of San Francisco, our state government. He'll take it all the way to the Supreme Court if necessary."

"The old criminal's complaint. Does the money even exist?"

"Probably Ordway has it, but there's no way anybody — not even our government — will be able to prove it or wrest it from him."

"This Macy — he confessed?"

"To any number of things; he just couldn't stop talking. Put it all on Renshaw: Gage planned the whole thing; Gage forced him into going along with his scam. Macy tried to stop him, but finally went along with him because of his crazy raving and threats of physical harm. There may be some truth in that; Macy certainly hopped to it every time Renshaw snapped his fingers. But from the tapes of their interview that the police let me listen to, Macy was definitely not a victim of Stockholm syndrome."

"And it was Macy who killed Adam Smithson?"

"Yes. He claims it was self-defense, that Smithson showed up just after he found the bonds and attacked him. Then he panicked and set the fire." I paused, then asked Hy about his exposure of Renshaw and Kessell to the CIA.

"It's all true. You saw my documentation."

"They never did anything about it. Do you think we should go public?"

Long silence. "Normally I'd say to let it be. M&R doesn't need any more exposure in the media than we've already had. But in this case, a hell of a lot of prominent people and corporations worldwide got away with heinous acts. None that were named in those documents were ever prosecuted or even sanctioned. Some are probably still going about bad business as usual in places like Iran and Iraq."

I'd been thinking along the same lines. "So we go public. How?"

"I've got a contact who's pretty high up at the *New York Times.* And you're in tight with the *Chronicle.*"

"One of my old college friends is an op-ed writer for the *Washington Post.* And my high-school friend Linnea Carraway recently moved from the Pacific Northwest to New York, where she hosts a syndicated talk show."

"And then there's the Internet."

"The Internet. YouTube. Twitter. Bloggers. Yes!"

"We'll have to go about it very carefully. Consult good lawyers."

"We can do it."

"Forward into battle."

"Amen to that."

■ ■ ■ ■

MONDAY, OCTOBER 26

■ ■ ■ ■

8:21 a.m.

There was a crowd gathered outside the M&R building when I arrived. I whipped my car into the underground parking garage and took the elevator to the ground floor.

"What the hell is going on?" I asked Lex, the guard at the double street doors.

"There's been an accident."

It must not have been much of an accident, because he was smiling.

"Look out there," he added, motioning toward the glass.

Six or seven large pieces of concrete lay on the pavement, and dust wafted above them in the sunlit air. The edges of the largest pieces were curved, like the edges of . . .

"The clamshell?" I asked Lex.

He nodded, and I started to smile too.

"How long ago?" I asked.

"Oh, maybe fifteen minutes. Big crash, almost scared me to death."

"Nobody was hurt, I hope?"

"Nobody was around."

"Nobody?"

"Yeah, nobody."

"Right."

"Right."

I pushed through the doors and skirted the wreckage. Studied it. Irreparable. Then I looked up at the gaping place where it had been attached to the building's wall. No structural damage; the wall shouldn't be too difficult to repair.

A hand touched my arm. Laura Banks, a reporter for the *Chronicle,* whom I knew reasonably well. "What happened here, Sharon?"

"I guess the installation was faulty."

"But it was a Flavio St. John installation. He's known for his perfection. When he finds out what's happened he's going to be livid."

I was looking beyond her to where two men in dusty work clothing stood grinning at me.

"Well, everyone makes a mistake sometimes, and I can't say I'm sorry about this one." I raised my voice as I added, "That sculpture was as ugly as my husband's aunt Stella Sue's butt."

Then I excused myself and went to join Hy and John.

ABOUT THE AUTHOR

Marcia Muller has written many novels and short stories. She has won six Anthony Awards, a Shamus Award, and is also the recipient of the Private Eye Writers of America's Lifetime Achievement Award as well as the Mystery Writers of America Grand Master Award (their highest accolade). She lives in northern California with her husband, mystery writer Bill Pronzini.